THE LIGHT OF REASON

The Director paced over to the window, standing with his arms folded behind his back, gazing outward, as if too embarrassed to face Richard.

"Of course it's all nonsense. Probably die down in a few months. But as things stand, the people in London think it might be a good idea if you took an indefinite leave of absence. Stay away from the lab. A sabbatical, if you like." He turned around. "In the States, perhaps?"

"You mean as far away from here as possible?"

The Director spread his hands in a gesture of helpless resignation.

"What about Cobb?"

"There doesn't seem to be quite so much bad feeling about John. He hasn't, after all, been sounding off on TV."

A light dawned on Richard.

"You mean, *one* of us has to be given to the wolves, and since I'm not the one who's bringing a fat contract from industry into the Institute, I get the short straw."

The Director frowned, and pressed a button to open the door to his outer office. His secretary stood there, ready for orders.

"Sir?"

"Dr. Lee will be taking the rest of the day off, Carol. The police should be here"—he glanced at the old-fashioned watch he wore on his left wrist—"in about five minutes, to see there's no trouble outside." He turned to Richard. "I took the liberty, Dick. Assumed you wouldn't want to drive your car after what that mob did to it."

BEN BOVA'S DISCOVERIES

BECOMING ALIEN by Rebecca Ore
NAPOLEON DISENTIMED by Hayford Peirce
ETHER ORE by H. C. Turk

BEN BOVA PRESENTS

THE THIRTEENTH MAJESTRAL by Hayford Peirce
BEING ALIEN by Rebecca Ore
PHYLUM MONSTERS by Hayford Peirce

BEN BOVA Presents Father To The Man

John Gribbin

A TOM DOHERTY ASSOCIATES BOOK
NEW YORK

FATHER TO THE MAN

Copyright © 1989 by John Gribbin

A TOR Book
Published by Tom Doherty Associates, Inc.
49 West 24 Street
New York, NY 10010

Cover art by David Mattingly

ISBN: 0-812-53850-1   Can. ISBN: 0-812-53851-X

First edition: February 1990

Printed in the United States of America

0 9 8 7 6 5 4 3 2 1

Prologue:
EXODUS

One

Year One

Housing was still cheap in Norfolk. The recent
run of severe cold winters, with winds howling
in from the east across the North Sea, bearing
their burden of snow, was in no measure com-
pensated for by the increasing warmth of the
summers, since that warmth seemed to bring
with it, more and more as the years went by, a
drifting, light but persistent rain. The farmers
complained bitterly, as farmers have always
complained, come rain or shine, from time im-
memorial. It was bad for the crops, they would
say, shaking their heads—and worse for the
livestock. The only thing that kept their heads
above water was the subsidy from the EEC.
Then they would depart, still gloomy, in their
late-model Jaguars or Land Rovers, and every
summer the news would carry stories of moun-
tains of food of one kind or another, stored

away in warehouses at great cost as a result of the European common agricultural policy.

The same news, of course, carried the stories and pictures of the starving in Africa, South America, and the East.

The farmers, in fact, couldn't afford to leave the land, thanks to their subsidies. Anyone else who got an opportunity to move south and west leaped at the chance, even if the cost were the ruinous mortgage they would be burdened with in trading upward in price, but downward in quality, from a large, comfortable old house near Norwich to a modern box in a housing development south of London. Which was how the old former vicarage, on the outskirts of town, came to acquire a new owner.

It seemed a little large for one man on his own, with its five bedrooms and the converted coach house standing in the grounds of more than an acre. But he had the money, and he was respectable enough—something to do with the university, though it was never clear exactly what—and the sellers were glad, in their own words, "to find a mug and get out while the going was good."

The conversion work on the building was a minor talking point in the nearby village for a week or two. The repairs to the high wall, now topped off with barbed wire; the refurbishment of the coach house; the computer and other equipment installed in the workshop cum laboratory of what soon became known as "the Professor's" house. But people soon had other things to interest them and gossip about. The election, in which the government, as predicted, returned to power with a reduced majority, but nothing seemed to change. The weather, which, according to the old men in the pubs, was always the worst they'd ever known. And if the Professor seemed to have a strange taste in pets, well, that certainly explained some of the work on the grounds and the coach house.

Within a few months, the Professor was accepted as a part of the surroundings. Quiet, keeping to himself, occasionally dropping in to the pub for a pint and a sandwich, but mostly either shut away in the house or off in Norwich, doing whatever it was he did at the university. He left people alone, and people left him alone, in the time-honored English tradition.

Two

It was the hot patch of sunlight, creeping round the room, angling through the loosely fitting curtain, that woke her. She raised a hand to cover her eyes, automatically, half conscious. The dirty sleeping bag that had covered her fell to the floor, revealing, if anyone had been there to see, the painful thinness of her limbs and body, flat-chested, almost sexless, dressed in a T-shirt almost as grubby as the sleeping bag. Both arms and the upper part of each leg were marked with livid, purple-black bruises, in stark contrast to the pale white of the surrounding skin. Perhaps—almost certainly—the girl/woman (her age was almost impossible to guess from her appearance) had once been pretty. Perhaps—just possibly—she could be pretty again.

Her tongue felt as if it filled her mouth to

overflowing, and tasted like a carpet covered in cigarette ash. She licked her dry lips, experimentally, but found no relief. Swinging her legs to the floor, she sat up, then leaned forward, head flat on her knees, as a wave of dizziness passed across her. Christ, she thought, I need a hit. Where the hell's Tom? Lifting her head again, experimentally, and balancing the weight of her body by leaning on the bed with her right arm, she watched the curtain as it seemed to ripple and wave, moving toward her and away again, as her eyes and brain tried to adjust to the reality of the room.

How the hell had she got into this mess? Tomorrow, she promised herself (as she did every day), she'd get the place cleaned up a bit, put on a dress and go round to the college. She wasn't sure just how long it had been since she last went in, but she knew she could make up the lost ground. Hell, it was her final year, after all. She'd done all the real work. Just got to take a couple of interviews, a written paper, piece of cake. Then she'd be a qualified nursery nurse, and she'd get a job, and she wouldn't have to depend on Tom for the stuff, and anyway she didn't really need it, much. But she could *really* use a hit just now, just to get her up. Where the hell was he?

An adrenaline flush took her to her feet and across to a table, littered with dirty coffee mugs and a McDonald's carton still containing a partly eaten cheeseburger and some cold french fries. Experimentally, she lifted one of them to her mouth, then dropped it back on the table. An empty polythene bag, smeared with traces of white powder, and a hypodermic sy-

ringe, its needle crusted with a rusty scar of
dried blood, were among the clutter. Energy
suddenly drained, she stood at the table, supporting herself with both arms, hands gripping
its edge tightly, head down, while she was
wracked by a fit of coughing.

Christ, if only she had a hit, she'd walk out of
here, before Tom came back. If she could just
get straight, she'd be out of here, for good. And
if he tried to come after her—well, she knew
enough about him to keep him out of her way,
and anyone else's for that matter, for a good ten
years. Christ, it'd be worth going down herself
just to see his face when they busted him. Just
one good hit, and a couple of hours to herself.
That's all she wanted.

When the door opened, she'd slumped to the
floor, shivering, but still holding herself upright
by the leg of the table. She didn't notice the
sound of the door, or the cool draft of wind. But
the voice registered, and she looked up as he
spoke.

"Still here, then?"

"Tom! Christ, where were you? I need a hit,
I need it now, c'mon ..."

Vaguely, she took in Tom's companion. A
short, dark girl. She looked familiar. Maybe
she'd met her in college. Who was she? What
was she doing here? The expression on the in-
truder's face suggested something was not quite
right in the room. But Tom was talking again.

"Pamela." He said it slowly and carefully, as
if talking to a small child. "Pamela, this is Liz.
You will be nice to Liz, won't you?"

He turned to the dark girl. "Look, I'm sorry

about this, Liz. Pam was supposed to have the place cleaned up a bit. But I guess she overslept. Maybe she isn't feeling too well."

Liz seemed largely unconcerned. Pam, rising unsteadily to her feet, still using the table for support, got a good look at her face, and realized why. The pupils of her eyes were so small they were practically invisible, leaving a bright blue pair of irises with no dark centers. Shit! Tom had got the stuff, and he'd been giving it to this bitch, instead of to her. She turned, reaching for his arm.

"Tom, please." She smiled. He'd always said how much he liked her smile. "Just a small one, huh? Then I'll get the place cleaned up, I promise."

He smiled back, but only with his mouth.

"Well, I dunno. It's hardly worth bothering. Me 'n' Liz, we can cope. P'rhaps you'd best just get dressed and get back to your own place. We'd like to be alone for a while, anyway."

His arm was round Liz's waist, possessively. She leaned against him, head nestled in the crook of his shoulder, obviously now largely oblivious to her surroundings. The penny finally dropped for Pam. Liz—this slut—this, this . . . Her brain could find no words. This *person* was *her* replacement. She sank back on the bed, trying to puzzle it out. What had happened when she first came here with Tom, was it six weeks ago (or six months)? Hadn't there been another girl around for a time, before she moved out and left the two of them to get on with it? There was a strange feeling of déjà vu about the whole scene, if only she could get it straight in her head, but with her role very different from last time. Hell, it didn't matter. All she needed was a hit and she'd be in control.

"Tom, please. Just give me the stuff. Just a tiny bit. Then I'll get my clothes together. Hey, I can get back to my place, easy . . . if you just give us a small hit. Please?"

He relented.

"Okay, baby." He kissed Liz, thoroughly, as if establishing his possession of her, and steered her into the one comfortable chair. "Just wait there, Liz, while I help Pam get her things together." He pulled a plastic bag from his jeans, and turned back to Pam. "Here it is, baby. Just a little one, okay? For old times. Then you'll be a good girl and run along back to your place?"

"Sure, Tom." Her eyes were fixed on his hands, as he began to prepare the shot. She'd do anything he said, as long as she got the hit. God, it was almost worth the waiting, now she could see it coming and imagine how good it was going to be. She giggled. She couldn't *wait* to see the expression on his face . . .

Three

Year Two

Unemployment was still high—touching five million in Britain alone. Jobs were hard to come by, and anyone lucky enough to get a congenial post in a private home, with flexible hours and no really arduous duties, would have been crazy to risk instant dismissal by blabbing to the world at large about those things that her employer preferred to be kept discreet—especially if her own past contained secrets she'd rather not talk about.

"Our client, Ms. Barnett, is a respectable, wealthy man. He has his own reasons for requiring privacy, and he is offering a good salary. We have not pried into those reasons—"

I bet you haven't, she thought at the interview. You don't want to lose your commission.

"—but I don't think I would be betraying any

confidences if I hinted at a romantic involve-
ment, the recent death of our client's companion." The client had, in fact, directed the agency
to say as much. That was his privilege; he was
paying the piper, after all.

"While respecting both his privacy and yours,
we have, of course, informed him that we have
every confidence in your own discretion."

In other words, Pam thought, with a momen-
tary flash of bitterness, you've told him I've got
a record. Then the anger passed. Well, she'd
known this would happen. Any employer was
bound to ask why someone with her nursing
background would be willing to take a job in
the sticks, even if it was well paid. And she
should have guessed that the prospect might actually appeal to someone who had his own reasons for lying low. But the interviewer was
continuing, and the moment of self-pity passed
as quickly as the anger that had preceded it.

"Now, the job involves living in, so you won't
be seeing much of the bright lights. On the other
hand,"—the interviewer glanced at the screen
of the terminal, in front of her—"it is rather
unlikely that any of your former contacts in
London will be bothering you up in Norfolk."

That was the clincher. Six months in prison—
they called it hospital, but it still had bars on
the windows and locked doors—six months inside had been bad enough, and she was determined not to get caught up in that mess again.
Thank God the HIV had still been in the quies-
cent phase and they'd been able to knock it out
of her system; she had that to thank them for—
and more. Tom had got five years. Even allowing for time off for good behavior, she'd be lost

in the country before he got out. She shivered again, remembering the threats he had hurled at her across the courtroom as he'd been dragged away. And, of course, she leaped at the opportunity being offered to her.

She never regretted it. At first, it seemed so obvious why the Professor wanted his privacy, and why he hid the baby from the world. If that was all he had left, after his wife (or was she his wife? Pam was never quite sure) had died, no wonder he wanted both to hide and to protect it from the world. Not that he ever talked about the past, or offered any explanations. Her duties were described, the contract was signed, specifying instant dismissal if news of any of the work going on leaked out, and she'd moved in the following week.

The Professor's "housekeeper" was young enough—certainly much younger than him—to cause some comment and gossip in the village at first, but she knew when she was well off, and kept out of the circle of rumor mongers, not even bothering to deny the allegations which were bound to be made. In a way, she was flattered by the attention. She was, however, as eager as the Professor to avoid gossip. Why shouldn't he have his privacy? There was nothing illegal involved, as far as she knew, and if there *was* anything illegal involved, she didn't want to know.

She'd been assured there were no extracurricular duties expected of her, and her employer had certainly been most correct in that department, almost old-fashioned. No hanky-panky. Sometimes, she almost wished there was. The Professor wasn't at all bad looking, really, and he certainly wasn't short of a few bob. It was, she knew, income from something he'd invented. Enough income that he didn't have to work on anything he didn't want to any more, but could do his own thing. If he was that clever, maybe he'd invent something else to make a bigger fortune, and maybe then he'd cheer up and decide he needed some real female companionship. Well, a girl could dream, couldn't she?

Four

Year Four

Guns and tanks were increasingly rare in the fighting in East Africa; combatant aircraft had vanished from the skies. Not because of any belated reluctance on the part of the so-called developed nations to supply military equipment to the embattled tribes—and nobody pretended any more that this was anything other than tribal skirmishing—but because the opposing forces simply didn't have any means to pay for weaponry on the world markets.

Once, colonial powers might have taken advantage of the opportunity to move in. But for what? Simply painting the map pink, or blue, or green, no longer seemed a fruitful exercise, and with agriculture down the tubes, hostile natives and no resources to speak of, the increasingly arid region lacked attractions for even the

most expansionist of governments farther
north.

White faces were still seen, in and around the
refugee camps, but seldom up-country. And the
trickle of aid did little to alleviate the problems
in the camps.

Maria's baby was dying. She sat in the scrap
of shade provided by the wall around the camp,
unmoving in the heat of the afternoon, while
flies crawled restlessly over the faces of herself
and her child, seeking the trace of moisture
around their lips and nostrils, even approaching their eyes, only to be scattered, briefly, by
a blink. Three years old, but scrawny, with a
large, seemingly overlarge, head and wasted
limbs, carrying the potbelly of malnutrition, the
baby still tried, occasionally, to suck sustenance from its mother's breast. But Maria, almost equally thin, surviving on the daily ration
of gruel issued by the aid agency, was scarcely
able to keep her own body alive, let alone provide sustenance for another.

What did it matter? She'd been a good girl,
an orphan named and raised by the Catholics
who ran a home for waifs and strays. There'd
been plenty of children like her, in the after-
math of the bloody years following Amin's fall,
but for a time something approaching peace
was established, and her life had been far from
hard, by the standards of the region. She'd been
ten when the latest government decided to kick
out all foreigners, and the school was closed.
Under that short-lived regime, forced return to
village life had been the order of the day, and
she had adapted reasonably well, quietly keeping her head down and out of trouble. But that

regime, like its predecessors, and its successors, hadn't lasted.

As countries created in the middle of the twentieth century by retreating colonial powers began to split apart and revert to tribal groupings, with no real pretense of a central, organized government any more, successive waves of soldiery passed through the village, looting, stealing hard-won food, taking the women they chose, before passing on and leaving the villagers to pick up the pieces. Maria had been thirteen when one group of five self-styled guerrillas, armed with three rifles, a handful of ammunition, two spears and one bow, on the run from a much larger force of opponents, had taken a fancy to her.

She had known what to expect, having seen the inevitable happen many times in the previous three years. She had seen that struggling and resistance ended, as often as not, in death—*after* the men had satisfied themselves. So she made no protests, never struggled, and tried hard not to cry out as each of the ragged band, most of them little older than herself, laughingly enjoyed her body. As a reward, she had been left alive, and pregnant.

Now, the village life was gone. The baby was dying, and she didn't know why she had bothered to look after it for three years, anyway. Nothing mattered. Perhaps, soon, she would die herself. As the sun moved across the sky, diminishing the patch of shade, the flies began to crawl back towards and across the baby's unblinking eyes.

* * *

Far to the north, another three-year-old sat on a young woman's lap, watching, bright-eyed, as she turned the pages of a glossy picture book. Pam felt a glow of pride and affection as the odd-looking little boy eagerly responded to each picture as it appeared. "Dog!" he cried out, happily, pointing at the picture. The page turned. "Horse!" Another page. "Cat!" If anyone had tried to tell her he was ugly, she simply wouldn't have believed them—although she did still sometimes recall, with slight embarrassment, her own initial reaction on seeing the infant. Better if he'd died at birth—the thought had flashed, unbidden, into her mind, quickly suppressed, and afterward acting as a spur to her to achieve as much as possible with the poor little creature. Only now, she didn't think of Adam as a poor little creature. He was hers, as near as made no difference, and she was the only mother he'd ever known, whatever the Professor chose to call her. If Adam could talk intelligently, by the standards of a three-year-old, and was beginning to understand the significance of printed words, it was to her credit as much as his. Maybe he wouldn't fit in with the outside world—yet—but if she had anything to do with it, he'd grow up into a healthy, intelligent young man. And long before then, she was sure, she would persuade the Professor to allow her to take Adam out to school. The old boy was definitely mellowing, even though he still kept himself very much to himself, and it did seem most natural to think of him as the Professor.

The boy was closing the book, looking round for another amusement.

"Very good, Adam." She smiled, proudly. "Where's the cat?"

The infant stabbed at the book with his finger. "Cat."

"No, not that cat. Where's Lucky?"

He looked around the room, quickly, alertly, and spotted the black and white animal curled up on a cushion in a patch of sunlight under the window. He pointed, yelling happily, "Cat! Lucky cat!"

She hugged him, and kissed him on the head. "Want an apple?" she asked.

"Yes. Apple?"

"Okay. But first, we play a game. First you put the pieces in your puzzle box, then you get an apple. Okay?"

Adam nodded, jumping down from the chair and running across the room to open a low cupboard. Inside, among a jumble of toys, was a large plastic ball, faceted with ten flat sides, that rattled when he pulled it out. He ran back to the woman, and sat down on the floor. Deftly, his small hands pulled the ball apart in two halves, tugging against the spring that held them together. Ten differently shaped pieces fell out—a cross, a triangle, a circle, and others. Each piece corresponded to a hole cut in one face of the ball. The two halves of the ball snapped back together as he released his grip, and concentrated on sorting through the pieces.

Frowning slightly in concentration, his tongue occasionally licking out of the corner of his lips, he fitted the pieces into the holes, trying them in different ways until they fell back inside the ball.

He half muttered to himself as he worked at

the task. "This one . . . In here . . . Another
one . . . In here . . . No . . . In here . . . Where is
it? . . . Square . . . Round one . . . In here . . ."

Soon he was finished and looked up, grinning
broadly. "Done! All gone! Apple now?"

She smiled, equally broadly, and reached
down to ruffle his hair with one hand, pulling a
green, crunchy apple from a pocket with the
other.

"Good boy! Here's your apple."

The cat stirred, lazily, in its pool of sunlight,
and stretched out its paws as it lay on its side.
Carefully, delicately, it began licking down one
leg, with repeated movements of its head and
tongue, while the child crunched happily on his
apple and the woman, still smiling, sat in the
chair, watching him. Thank God she'd found
this refuge.

Five

The fires that raged across eastern parts of Australia, worse even than those of 1983, were the result of drought—the most severe drought ever recorded in Australian meteorological history (which, admittedly, only went back a little over a hundred years). The climatologists nodded wisely, and said that this confirmed what they had known for ten years, that the features of the southern ocean called the Southern Oscillation and El Niño were responsible for hemisphere-wide flips in the weather, from one condition to another. They pointed to the 110 millimeters of rain at Guayaquil in Ecuador in the single month of November, compared with a normal figure of 8 mm, and the record single-month rainfall, of 723 mm, at the same site two months later in January, as ample confirmation of their theories. It wasn't that the Australian rainfall had disappeared, they pointed out, but rather that rains which belonged in the western Pacific were weak while those that belonged in the eastern Pacific were strong. It would all average out in the long term.

Devastation across one-third of Ecuador, with widespread loss of life, property damage, and economic disruption was, however, short-term and immediate. In Melbourne, although firefighters beat back the flames before they could do more than lick the edge of the city suburbs, the sky was dark with the pall of smoke from raging bushfires for three days in February, and the temperature peaked out at 45.7 degrees Centigrade, the highest ever recorded there. The rice crop crashed to 57 percent of its usual production, and the wheat harvest, at 6.8 million tons, was only 30 percent of the expected yield. The long term didn't do any more good to Australian farmers put out of business and left homeless by the fires than it did to South American peasants drowned in the floods.

When pressed, even the climatologists agreed that something unusual might be going on. They muttered darkly about the increase in annual rainfall of more than 100 mm that occurred across Victoria, New South Wales, and Queensland between 1946 and 1974, when the world as a whole had been cooling slightly. And they acknowledged that, since the world had now been warming up for the best part of twenty years, the decline in rainfall might well be long-term, if not permanent. It was all, they said, probably due to the greenhouse effect—a buildup of carbon dioxide in the atmosphere, trapping heat, and caused by humankind's greedy consumption of oil and coal, not to mention the destruction of the tropical rain forest of Brazil. Chlorofluorocarbons and other compounds essential to the modern world played their part. So what could be done? Human civilization and the greenhouse effect went hand in hand; halt one, and you'd stop the other dead in its tracks, too.

Why worry, anyway, said the optimists. A warmer world might be a nicer place to live in. And devotees of the burgeoning Gaia cult took comfort in their view of the ecosystem of the earth as a single living organism, a benevolent earth mother working for the good of all to maintain conditions suitable for life on Earth. They ignored, if they were ever aware of, the remark once made by Jim Lovelock, father of the Gaia hypothesis. "Gaia," he'd said in a video interview, "isn't out to protect mankind, she's out to protect herself. Maybe the best way for Gaia to protect herself is to get rid of the irritations being caused by human activities."

The interviewer, walking into the trap, had responded, "How could she do that?"

And Lovelock, smiling his patient smile, had quietly said, "The same way that you would stop the irritation caused by mosquitoes."

Question and answer never made the broadcast version of the tape, but had been one of the highlights of the bootleg collection that made the rounds of the studios that Christmas, showing all the fluffs and screwups, over the past year, and, best of all, the smooth, slick front man for once completely wrong-footed by his intended victim.

In Europe, civilization proceeded pretty much

as before. The funny weather didn't have very much effect on crops in that favored, temperate region of the globe. A little more rain here for a few summers; a little less rain there. Certainly not worth cutting back on the amount of coal and oil being burned in power stations and factories; the "cure" would, in economic terms, be worse than the disease. Besides, if the change in climate *was* a result of human activities, human ingenuity would find a solution. Wouldn't it? Even the ponderous machinery of the European agricultural program was able to cope with the changes so far. And the harvest failures in other parts of the world were quite useful, really, since they enabled the administrators to get rid of some of the politically embarrassing surpluses, if only as food aid. The Australian bushfires, and the floods in South America, were, for most people, simply something to gawp at on the screen, secure in the knowledge that it couldn't happen here.

"Madam President." Peter Beckman swallowed nervously, his prominent Adam's apple bobbing in his long, thin throat. "I very much appreciate the honor—"

"Let's cut out the crap, Dr. Beckman." Alice Christie, the short, dark woman on the other side of the desk, hadn't got where she was today by bothering too much about the niceties in what was still a male-dominated society. "You've got something important to tell me about the population crisis. It must be important, or my advisers wouldn't insist on my seeing you. But I've read your report—" she gestured at a screen inset into her desk—"and

what I understand of it is crazy. You've got
about ten minutes to persuade me to take you
seriously."

"But—" Beckman couldn't resist a glance at
his watch. Ten minutes! It had taken him the
best part of ten years to come up with the theory. But this was his only chance to put it across
where it counted. He swallowed again, and tried
to get a grip on himself. "As you wish. It's really
all about the demographic transition—what
happens to the breeding pattern of people when
their economic circumstances change."

"That much I do understand, Dr. Beckman,"
the President responded dryly. "The econo-
mists have been telling us for years that if we
provide enough aid to the third world to improve their living standards, then people will
only choose to have two children per family.
The trouble is, we can't seem to provide the aid
as fast as they breed."

"Exactly." Perhaps things were going to go
smoothly after all. She did *seem* to have some
grasp of what was going on. "Its like this. In
nature, there are two successful breeding strat-
egies. Some species produce enormous quanti-
ties of offspring, so that at least a few survive
to breed in their turn. Others produce only a
few offspring, and devote a lot of effort to making sure that each of them survives to become
an adult. It turns out that the first strategy is
best for species who really have to struggle to
survive, who live in a crowded ecological
niche—as a parent, you'd be gambling a small
amount on a lot of different options. Even if the
parent doesn't survive, the offspring are in with
a chance. But the second strategy is best when

pickings are easy. If you are sure of your food
supply, or whatever, then it makes sense to
make a big investment on one or two offspring
that you know you can nurture."

He glanced at his watch again. Seven minutes
left. Did she mean that deadline? Mentally, he
junked most of his prepared speech, and fell
back on his experience of talking to the news-
tapes.

"The thing is,"—Beckman was warming to his
task now—"the human animal is different. The
reason we've been so successful is that we can
adapt our breeding pattern to suit the circumstances. We aren't stuck with one pattern of behavior, programmed by evolution. In some
societies, we produce lots of children; in others
only a few. But always, instinctively, we produce as many as we can to use the available
resources."

"As many as we can?" The President seemed
surprised. "Surely the opposite is true. It's the
poor countries that are bulging at the seams,
and our problem is that we aren't replacing our
aging population, while our southern neighbors
are kicking in the door."

"No, no. Not at all. You miss the point. In a
poverty-stricken society, the standard of living
is low. It doesn't cost much more to raise six
children than to raise five. As soon as the children can walk, they start to work; as soon as
they are independent, they leave home. You can
always squeeze one or two more into the slums
of Mexico City. Life really is cheap there—the
standard of living is appalling, but it doesn't
cost much to maintain. But it's different up
here. How much did it cost your parents to put

you through college? We have more, so we *expect* more. Parents know that each child they have will be an economic burden for at least twenty-five years. Instinctively, they respond with the correct breeding pattern. A few children, each of them certain to grow up safely with the best food and medical attention, each of them requiring years of expensive education just to make sure they can get a job. *That* is what the demographic transition is all about. Anyone in our society who produces five or six children will be bankrupted trying to look after them in the manner expected. It's more efficient to raise a few children successfully. And that's why, if only we could raise the standards of our southern neighbors, their population problem would go away."

"And what of our population problem? The single-child family is distorting the whole economic base of the United States. How can fewer and fewer productive people support more and more pensioners? How can we make our people produce more children, before we become a geriatric nation swamped in the tide of illegal immigrants from the south?"

"I don't know. Things may have gone too far. What that report tells you"—it was Beckman's turn to nod at the viewscreen—"is that we are experiencing a second demographic transition. We have become too successful, too affluent for our own good. A family with even two children can't pay its way long enough for the children to get a decent education. So we have the single-child family. There are fewer youngsters, and more and more oldsters, who also have to be looked after. Soon, it won't make economic sense to have children at all. But the poor people from the south, with lesser aspirations, will happily move into our ecological niche. What I'm telling you, Madam President, is that our way of life is doomed. There is nothing you can do to save it."

"Nothing we can do to preserve our heritage? No way that the ideals preserved for more than two centuries can be maintained?"

"Oh, I didn't say that. I said no way to preserve *our* way of life. You could preserve the ideals enshrined in the Constitution, all right. You could even get back to the roots of our nation's strength, and make those ideals stronger than ever before. What you have to do is reduce our standard of living to that of the original pioneers. Move everyone out of the cities, and destroy them. Get back to a peasant society, dependent on agriculture, but where everyone is free, truly free, with no bureaucracy, no Internal Revenue Service, and no politicians. Where life is cheaper, but happier.

"But perhaps, Madam President, that isn't an *acceptable* solution?"

Boulder, Colorado, is far from being the most excitable city in the United States. But even there the speaker drew a crowd of thousands. They'd seen him on the screen, of course, so his pure white hair and lined, craggy features were already familiar. His message, too, was familiar. But it felt even more right heard in the flesh, face-to-face—as far as it could be face-to-face, in a baseball stadium with electronic voice amplification. In fact, the image makers who took such care to keep the hair snowy white were

also careful to fill the stadium with suitable
subsonics, to enhance the audience response.
But after all, the occasion was being broadcast
coast to coast, and everybody present left feeling uplifted, so what harm was being done?

The message was familiar, and it was com-
forting.

"My friends." He spread his arms wide, in the
familiar, all-embracing gesture.

"You all know why I have come here today,
to speak directly to you. Our great nation is in
trouble, more trouble than it has been in since
our noble ancestors threw off the colonial yoke.
Honest men cannot find work; their children
have no prospects. Criminals walk the streets
of our cities, unchecked as they go about their
evil business. And why? Where have we gone
wrong?

"We are being punished, my friends. Punished, because we have turned our backs on
God, and have lost our way.

"No!" Raising one hand high, then bringing it
down in a dramatic gesture. "We have not *lost*
our way! We have *chosen* the way of sin, be-
guiled by the false gods of science and technology, by our lust for the easy life. We may have
eased our material bodies, my friends"—his
voice dropping to what seemed like a conspiratorial whisper, though still clearly audible to
every person in the stadium, and the vast TV
audience—"but at what cost to our immortal
souls?"

That was just the beginning. He had them eating out of the palm of his hand. The need for a
return to the pioneer values of simplicity and
the family, the need to cry halt to the rampant

march of science, especially the hubris of scientists who claimed to be able to improve on God's creation, the human body. And, almost as an afterthought, the need to keep the country pure, sealing off its borders against the tidal wave of immigration from those who were even more distanced from God than the blessed inhabitants of the greatest nation on earth.

Then, his local mission completed, the subsonics and the psychology having done their trick yet again, the amplified voice and image having been bounced by satellite into the homes of millions of ordinary people, the evangelist of the pioneering way of life and his entourage packed up and left, in their private jet, for the next engagement.

"That man has got to be stopped, Jeff."

The aide shrugged. "But how?"

"D'you think Beckman could be right? Are we really seeing the collapse of our civilization?"

"Ma'am, I don't know. But if it's any comfort, we aren't the only ones with the problem. Look at this." He handed her a printout.

REUTERS, London. Spokesmen for the extreme right-wing parties in Britain, Germany, France, and Spain announced today the formation of a new, European party, the United Front. The common goals of the four national parties, said a spokesman today, made it logical for them to join together in a common cause. In spite of the differences between them, they all agreed on the immediate priority of halting the flow of non-

European immigrants into the European community.

Pierre Chasseaud, former President and leader of the French Socialist Party, responded to the news with the comment, "This simply shows that the neo-Nazis are on the run. Because they have been reduced to tiny rumps in their own countries, they have to huddle together for support. We have nothing to fear from their so-called United Front." ENDS

"Is Chasseaud right?"

The aide smiled. "You know Chasseaud. Always whistling in the dark. With their proportional representation system, the UF is bound to win seats in the next European elections. If they got enough seats—well, remember Germany in the 1930s."

She shook her head. "This job doesn't get any easier, Jeff. Want to take over?"

He smiled again. "No, thank you, Madam President."

Six

Year Five

The sound of the warning siren echoed loudly round the deserted Embankment tube station. A rat, startled by the noise, scurried from its hiding place and ran along the rail, into the dark tunnel. One of the two uniformed men carrying out a last-minute check nudged his companion, and pointed after the rat.

"Shoudn't fancy 'is chances!"

His companion shouted back. "Us neither, if we don't"—the siren stopped, and the rest of his words boomed forth in the sudden quiet—"get out ourselves."

They passed through a low archway, and waved at the TV camera. Two levels higher, in a dimly lit control room, the technician watching the bank of monitor screens picked up a hand microphone.

"All clear this end. Closing doors now."

He punched at a control, and watched in the monitors as a series of curved steel doors slid down from the roof and ground into place, sealing off the tunnels. One way to solve the rat problem, he thought to himself. But there'll be a hell of a mess to clear up in the morning. Well, time to go upstairs and watch the fun. The water level must be pretty high by now.

"What are we going to do about this, Frank?" The leader of His Majesty's Opposition tapped the slim folder on the desk. "Four weeks to polling day, and we're still running two points behind in the polls. The London marginals could be crucial in this election. We've been handed a gift, but we mustn't let it blow up in our faces."

Frank picked up the folder, and riffled through the sheets inside. Some were newspaper clippings or photocopies, with headlines reading "Minutes from disaster," "Thames barrier flaws put city at risk," "London's costly white elephant." Beneath them, a three-page summary outlined the near-disaster of five days previously, when one of the gates of the Thames flood barrier failed to close properly, and the river had burst over the Embankment for the first time since 1953.

He knew what they contained, but he was giving himself time to phrase his reply. A major disaster had failed to materialize only because the wind had veered to blow from the west, holding back the worst of the surge of water that had come rushing, with the storm depression, down the North Sea. Holland's great sea barrier on the Eastern Scheldt had been much more severely tested, and had passed the test with flying colors, doubling the embarrassment to the British authorities. But how to turn that embarrassment to advantage?

Frank was familiar with the material. "The equipment is simply out of date. Technology from the sixties and seventies. It still uses mechanical relays to control the machinery, and failures are bound to happen.

"I'm not sure how much mileage we can make out of this. Act of God, that sort of thing. And, as you say, if we try to use it as a stick to beat the government it might rebound. Making capital out of people's misery, that sort of thing. Their publicity machine could wipe us out on this one."

"I know, Frank, but we've got to do something. All right, successive governments have been negligent. But this one's been in power for ten years now. What's happened in the past ten years that they should have taken note of, and acted on, to make London safer from floods? After all, the barrier had to be used in anger three times in the past eight months alone. When it was built in the eighties, there was hardly one flood warning a year. Why is that?"

"Well, we've had more rainfall, more storms. The farming lobby will tell you that! And there's the sea-level rise—only about two centimeters, but that chap in Norwich is always getting steamed up about it. Says they're related. There's a briefing document here somewhere, the one about the 'anthropogenic greenhouse effect.' I see he's going to be on *This Week* tomorrow, talking about floods."

"Is he, indeed." An idea was forming, and the

man who desperately wanted to be the next Prime Minister of Great Britain made a note on his pad, doodling a succession of concentric circles around the words "farming" and "Norwich."

"If there were good scientific reasons to expect more frequent flood hazards, and they've been ignored, we could be on to something. And if the farmers are worried, and we can present ourselves as the party that is going to do something about these problems with the weather—well, there's a lot of votes in farming, Frank!" He smiled. "This could be it. What do you know about the professor from Norwich?"

Frank closed his eyes, briefly, leaning back in his chair and letting the phenomenal memory that made him such a vital assistant go to work. He opened them again.

"Name's MacRobyn. In his forties. Looks younger, good speaker. Very good on TV. He sent us a study on the changing climate, about two years ago. I'm afraid"—he looked embarrassed—"we ignored it."

"That doesn't matter." The omission was dismissed with a wave of the hand. "Just as long as everyone else ignored it then. I want a copy of that report, Frank, within the next hour. And I'd like to see Professor MacRobyn tomorrow—*before* he goes along to the *This Week* studios. Do you think he'll come?"

"Oh yes, sir. He's been trying to get political attention for his work for years. I don't know if he actually supports us, but he's been very hostile to the government over its neglect of environmental sciences. Offer him a bone, and I think he'll jump our way."

"Now Frank, let's not be opportunistic. The problem of climatic change is a serious environmental issue, as the recent near-disaster in London shows. The present government has been guilty of catastrophic neglect of a problem which could have far-reaching implications, not just for Londoners but for agriculture in Britain and Europe. It's caused by our own folly—burning coal, releasing these CFCs to the air, something we can take action on ourselves, and within the EEC. And all the time the government has had warning signals from one of our own scientific experts, a world authority, who has more respect outside Britain than in his own country."

"Yes, boss." Frank smiled. It was good to see the glint of battle back in the old man's eyes. Those damned opinion polls had been worrying, but now, they just might have an edge.

The change of government made no difference to Adam, and very little difference to anyone else. Employment in Norwich was boosted, briefly, by the construction work on the new tower of the climate research center. But anyone who'd expected a new broom to sweep away the problems of the past twenty years, be they social or environmental, was in for a disappointment.

Climatic and social changes, however, were just about the least thing Adam had to worry about, in his centrally heated, air-conditioned home. He never met anybody, except his Nanny and Uncle Dick, and knew nothing of outside society. Equally, he never traveled far enough outside to be bothered much by any kind of weather, and he got his exercise, like almost everything else he did, indoors.

Uncle Dick was good fun, even if he couldn't climb very well or run fast, like Adam. He was always thinking up new games to play and tricks for Adam to do, and as Adam had got bigger and stronger Dick had brought in new toys and equipment for him to play on. He liked it when the things were arranged to make an obstacle course, with some things to crawl through, and some to jump on, and ropes to swing from. He could get right round the gym, over, under, and through the obstacles, in less than two minutes, without touching the ground.

And, in a different way, he liked the delicate concentration involved in exercising on the beam, slowly and with precision, walking the narrow bar with back straight and going through a precisely controlled and planned-out routine. He'd watched videos of other people working through gymnastic routines, and tried to copy them. Of course, he wasn't as good as they, yet, but he was still growing up. Maybe Uncle Dick would let him be a gymnast, when he'd grown up properly.

Seven

Pam knew she was taking a gamble, but she felt there'd never be a better chance. Not really a gamble, she told herself; a calculated risk. If he blows up and bawls me out—well, we've had our disagreements before. He's not going to sack me now. We're too comfortable together.

Comfortable—like a married couple, in some ways, by now. They probably saw more of each other than most married couples did, come to that—except at bedtime. Still no hanky-panky, but maybe that was why they got along so well together. Dick worked in his lab some of the time, and went in to the university at longer and longer intervals, but most of his life seemed to be dedicated to bringing up Adam, or at least to watching her bring up Adam. She'd never really been happy about the one-way glass in the nursery, which he used as a window to watch

Adam, and her, without being observed. There'd been an argument over that, she recalled, and he'd won. But he clearly loved the boy, like a son. *Like* a son, but *not* a son. She'd soon appreciated that, although she'd never fathomed the relationship. Once Adam could talk, the Professor became Uncle Dick to him; she, at the Professor's insistence, was always Nanny to the boy, although the two adults had long been on first-name terms themselves.

She knew the stories that were told in the village, the rumors, fired no doubt by gossip from the various women who had come in as daily helps at one time or another. A Frankenstein monster; a wild man, captured in Africa and brought home by the Professor; even a visitor from another planet. None of the dailies had ever met Adam, of course; but they knew somebody, or something, lived in the low building next to the old house, and they delighted in telling each other modern ghost stories to pass the time. Of course, none of them really believed it. Professor Lee was a respectable, polite, if slightly aloof man, who paid good wages. The story most of the villagers placed most store in was the one about an idiot child, born brain damaged when the Professor's wife died. And although Pam was now certain that this could not be the truth—Adam, though he did look a little odd, was scarcely a retarded idiot or a victim of Down's syndrome—it was the story she did least to deny, when pressed by acquaintances in the shops or pub. And so, without telling any direct lies, she helped to foster the impression the Professor clearly wanted to give.

In her own mind, when she allowed herself to

consider such things, she inclined more toward the Frankenstein school of thought. The lab, the Professor's background in biological research, the reports she'd looked up, in old magazines and newspapers, on one of the visits to the university library that Professor Lee knew nothing about. It all added up. But she preferred not to think about it, or to take any action to rock the boat. Adam was happy. She loved the boy, and he responded in kind. Dick was indeed, to all intents and purposes, a benevolent uncle in charge of an orphaned close relation. Where could Adam, whatever his origins, get better attention? Who could look after him better than she did? And what chance would she have of keeping him if she went to the authorities (what authorities? maybe it wasn't even illegal!) with wild tales about the respectable Professor Lee, who had more degrees than anyone else she'd met, and a Nobel prize to boot?

There was only one snag. With Adam nearing five, she was increasingly convinced that he *had* to get out in the world and mix with other children. He had to be socialized, in the jargon of her unfinished training. But the Professor kept him incommunicado, and limited his knowledge of the outside world. Maybe that helped to keep Adam happy, for a time. But she and the Professor wouldn't live forever. He had to make his own way someday, and it was time he started to learn how. Which was why she'd gone to all this trouble tonight.

Dick was always in a good mood when he returned from a day at the university. Duty, or whatever it was, done for a time, with the prospect of weeks at home before he felt the obligation, or need, for another visit, he mellowed visibly. A special dinner—they often cooked for each other and ate together, but usually on a much more modest and mundane scale—some wine, now a glass of brandy with the coffee. Hell, she thought, I really *am* acting like a wife getting ready to ask a favor. Oh well, here goes.

She put the coffee cup down on the small table beside her chair.

"Dick . . ."

He looked up, quizzically, from the brandy he'd been swirling in the glass. Suddenly, he smiled broadly.

"Better spit it out, Pamela." He never used the diminutive. Sometimes, she wished he would.

"What?"

He made a brief snort, suppressing a laugh.

"Whatever it is you've got in mind. I'm not completely ignorant of the ways of feminine intrigue, you know. All this reminds me of something that happened long ago, with someone I used to know. You're up to something, something you think I might not approve of, and you're buttering me up. Well, you've done a good job. I guess we've gotten to know each other quite well over the past few years. I'd certainly hate to think anyone else knew just which buttons to press to put me in a good mood." The smile faded, his glance returned to the brandy. Quickly, he looked up again. "But since it's you, I guess I don't mind. Is it about Adam? I hope you aren't planning to leave us; I could probably run to more money, if that's—"

She held up a hand, stopping him before he went too far down the wrong track. Might've

known the clever devil would be wise to her
scheme.

"No, no. That's not it. I've got plenty—I live
here, I don't spend half what you pay me. No.

"But it is Adam. He's fine in himself. No com-
plaints. But there's something worrying me.
About his long-term future."

She looked straight into his eyes.

"Dick, I dont know *why* you keep Adam
locked away here. I'm not sure I want to know.
He's happy, I'm happy—why rock the boat? But
there's something you've got to face. He can't
be locked up forever. What happens when you
die? I mean, God forbid, not for ages yet, but
one day? Adam's pretty normal, considering.
More normal than you realize, maybe. But he's
never met another child, and only knows two
adults. We've got to start thinking about how to
introduce him to other kids his own age, and
getting him out into the world."

"Not yet." The strength of the flat refusal
brooked no argument. There was silence for a
moment, then he relented.

"You're right, of course. One day. But it's too
soon. Not too soon for him, but for me, and for
the world outside. If they only knew ..." He
sighed. "I can't live forever, but I should be
good for another twenty or thirty years. By then
attitudes are bound to change. These things go
in cycles ...

"On the other hand, I suppose I might get run
over by a bus next time I'm in Norwich." He
sipped the brandy, reflectively, then looked at
her again.

"Maybe you're ready for this. If you haven't
got any plans to move on just yet?"

She shook her head.

"My last contract expired eighteen months ago, Dick. But I'm still here."

He smiled. "That long? It must be love then—lucky Adam—certainly can't be my fatal charm." A decision had clearly been reached.

"Okay, then. Here goes. I've written a lot of this down, but you'll be the first person I've told the whole story to. Hear me out, then tell me if you still think we ought to set Adam loose on an unsuspecting world. Or even let them suspect." He stood.

"But it's a long story. Better let me top you up, first."

She held out her glass as he lifted the decanter from the table, wondering just what it was she had got herself into.

Part One
GENESIS

Eight

It had started, Dick supposed, on his return from that last visit to Africa, more than ten years before . . .

The incessant dripping of moisture from high in the foliage above him was a constant reminder of the alien nature of the environment. From down here on the ground, nobody could tell whether or not it was actually raining up above the treetops, and it didn't make any difference whether it was or not. Yesterday's rain or today's, it all merged into a constant stream, filtering down past the leaves, dripping from branch to branch, running down the trunks of the trees, and finally concentrating in a stream directed at his neck. Richard Lee tugged, futilely, at the light tropical jacket in an attempt to unstick its clammy embrace from his body.

Then he froze into stillness, motioning his companions to silence, as their quarry came into view.

He was well aware of the irony of his situation, not to mention the danger. Not danger from the immediate environment, or its inhabitants. He was well dosed up with anti-this and anti-that medication, and the jungle of Zaire housed no creatures that were a match for the weapons carried by the four men. No, the danger came from that most dangerous of all creatures, his fellow civilized human beings. If the park authorities, let alone the police, got an inkling of what he was up to, it wouldn't just be the end of his career, but inevitably five years in jail. A Zaire jail at that—the prospect was not an attractive one, and he dismissed it from his mind. This might be one of the few places left in Africa where a recognizable government was in control, but it was hardly a government modeled on Western democracy. The stakes were high, but the gamble was worth it. If this came off, nobody would care *how* he had obtained the information, and his name would live in the annals of science forever. And, of course, there was the more immediate practical point that he would very rapidly become enormously rich.

The target of all this activity scarcely looked worth the candle. A small group of hairy apes, perhaps a dozen in all, huddling together out of the rain in almost human fashion. There were probably less than two hundred members of the species left in the wild on earth, all of them resident in the block of jungle embraced by the great arc of the Zaire River. And he, a scientist dedicated to the preservation of life on earth, was going to remove one of them—a breeding female, at that. Well, they weren't long for this world anyway, he rationalized. The forests were being cut back for coffee plantations, the natives still hunted the chimpanzees for their meat, considered something of a local delicacy, in spite of the efforts of the understaffed, underfinanced park service, and poachers still raided the dwindling communities for the illegal export market into zoos and, yes, scientific laboratories. After all, a live chimpanzee could fetch five times as much, on the black market, as a plantation worker earned in a month. At least he was doing his own dirty work. He had to, to be sure of getting the specimen he wanted. And if his plans worked out, her genes would be around long after her species was otherwise extinct.

Anyway, over on the eastern side of the continent her cousins, the common chimpanzees, *Pan troglodytes*, seemed to be spreading. Twenty-five years of droughts, starvation, civil and tribal wars had left most of Africa in a mess, as far as human society was concerned. A hell of a lot of the wildlife was flourishing as a result—except, of course, in what was left of South Africa. But it was far too dangerous for someone like him to risk venturing into. They were back to spears and poison arrows, and none too choosy about who they used them on. So, *Pan paniscus* was the "volunteer" for this job, and it was just their hard luck that they were an evolutionary dead end.

He nodded to his companions, and gestured wide with both hands. They nodded back, spreading out on either side to cover as wide an arc as possible. Lee unslung the anesthetic rifle from his back, and looked carefully through the sight, selecting his victim. He had already chosen the strength of anesthetic, set on the darts for a body weight of twenty-five to thirty kilos, and there was a young female, a full meter in height, perhaps a little more, that looked just right. He fired, and she looked up, startled, as the dart stuck in her right shoulder. With an almost human gesture, she reached round with her left hand to tug at the irritating object, then slowly collapsed where she stood. His companions rushed in from either side, nets at the ready; her companions fled, chattering to themselves, deeper into the rain forest. The easy part of the job was over; now they had to smuggle her back to England. Fortunately, few officials outside the park itself would know the difference between the rare pygmy chimpanzee and its more common, legally exportable, cousin. And his papers gave him carte blanche to collect up to three specimens of good old *Pan troglodytes*.

The guard at the Institute for Biomolecular Research building scarcely glanced at Lee's pass before raising the barrier and letting him drive through. But still, he *was* a guard, and it *was* a barrier.

I'm getting old, Richard told himself, not for the first time. Guards and passes and barricades at the entrance to a university research building give me the creeps. I can understand it over on the park, where the industrial guys are busy cutting each others' throats, but who would've thought it here?

But, of course, the security wasn't designed to prevent industrial espionage. They had no secrets here—everything was published openly. That was the trouble. Since a few hotheads had taken it upon themselves to decide what kind of research was morally allowable, the lab had been put on the hit list of the more loony extremists in the Animal Liberation Front. Exaggerated tales of cruelty to animals, plus a hint of Frankenstein monsters, was enough to stir up an occasional demonstration rowdy enough to make the researchers happy to be behind the wire fence and the guards. But what a hell of a world to live in, when research designed to save human lives and suffering was at risk because of the antics of a vociferous minority too ignorant to know the difference between recombinant DNA and grave robbing.

He swung the green Renault Estate into his parking bay in front of the new, glass-walled building, double-checked that the hand brake was properly engaged, and tucked a shabby leather briefcase, its handle missing, under one arm as he slammed the car door behind him, without bothering to lock it. At the top of the short flight of steps, through the swinging glass doors, was another security man in his cubicle, an array of TV monitors flickering with a greenish light to one side.

"Hi, Joe. What's new?"

"Nothing much, Dr. Lee. United lost again. Lousy weather forecast for the weekend. And the professor's worried that they're going to cut our budget."

Richard grinned. Joe was a professional pessimist, who seemed to have the sole object in life of spreading bad news.

"Thanks, Joe. It's only the thought of your happy smiling face that gets me up in the morning."

He reached for the handful of letters in the pigeonhole with his name on, and flipped through them as he walked down the corridor. A few bits of junk—news of forthcoming conferences, reprint requests—and one addressed by hand in green ink. Bad sign, green ink. Usually an indication of some friend of the furry creatures complaining about research on animals. Oh well.

The door to his office—unlocked, like the car door—opened easily to the pressure of his elbow as he leaned on it, one hand full of letters and the other controlling the wayward briefcase. He dropped the briefcase on the leather chair next to his desk, the letters on the desk, and pulled the cord which turned on the fluorescent overhead lighting. Even in broad daylight, the stand of tall conifers just outside the window kept the office gloomy enough to need artificial lighting, especially in these overcast conditions that seemed to persist for weeks on end.

Still standing, Richard sliced open the letters with a paper knife, dropping the contents, and the envelopes, one by one into the metal waste bin. Then, frowning slightly, he bent down and retrieved the two reprint requests. Better not be churlish. The Institute's secretaries could send out some copies of the papers easily enough, after all. Though Richard was convinced that people who sent out for copies of scientific papers never really read them, but collected them like stamps. If you were really working in the field, you'd pick up all the hot news at conferences months before it was published, and you'd probably photocopy the papers you needed straight out of the journals, whatever the copyright laws said. The only requests he always honored were those from third world countries where there probably was a shortage of funds for travel to international conferences, and a shortage of photocopiers. It helped to assuage a kind of vague postcolonial guilt he felt, as a white European, one of the haves, in a world where most people were have-nots.

Leaning across the swivel chair behind the desk, and resting his weight on his left hand, he punched a code into the computer terminal and quickly scanned the list of electronic mail items deposited since he had logged off the night before. Nothing much—except one from Marjorie. The push of another key brought the item up on the screen:

DICK
I'VE GOT A PROPOSAL TO PUT TO YOU. HOW ABOUT
LUNCH IN COLLEGE?
LOVE, M.

At last, he pulled the chair out from the desk and sat in it, swiveling to grab the briefcase and rummaging through it for a dog-eared pocket diary. Nothing much else on. Lunch it was, with Marjorie. Quickly, he tapped at the keys, using only his large right hand, which easily spanned the keyboard. The left, he always assured astonished professional typists mystified by his self-taught technique, was a spare, for use only in emergencies, or for picking his nose. The acceptance of Marjorie's invitation was soon filed in her own terminal, out at the primate research center. Not that Marjorie was likely to be there, of course. Lunch in town meant she was probably in Cambridge already, but no doubt she'd check her mailbox from wherever she happened to be.

Time for work. Well, nearly. He checked his watch. Ten-thirty, near enough. Time for coffee, then a chat with Cobb over at the lab, then lunch. Richard was a slow starter, and seldom got anything worthwhile done in the mornings. But if things were going well in the lab, he'd been known to work right through the night, or several straight nights. When things were going badly, he could be the prince of procrastination.

Nine

Marjorie was waiting in the Senior Common Room, sitting in one of the large, old over-stuffed chairs, reading, or at least flipping through, the pages of *Nature*. He flopped down in the chair beside her, stretching his long legs out under the small table.

"Hi. Ready to eat?"

She closed the journal and placed it carefully on the table.

"As ready as I'll ever be." Her quick, bright smile was replaced immediately by a serious expression. She hunched forward in her chair, bringing her face closer to him, and spoke quietly.

"Dick, can we get one of the side tables? I don't want to spend the next hour talking about college finances and the appalling standard of this year's undergraduate intake."

So she *was* serious about having something to discuss. The side tables were a new and daring innovation, introduced on a trial basis only six years ago, in a college which had a proud history going back to the fourteenth century. As the world moved inexorably toward the last decade of the twentieth century, and began to plan for the twenty-first, the council had reluctantly given way to pressure from the large number of scientific Fellows in the college, and consented to the introduction of a few small tables in Hall where, at lunchtime only, it was permitted to talk shop. It wasn't approved, that was made clear, but it was permitted, provided it wasn't done too often. And it was, of course, only a trial measure, which would be reviewed shortly—in another decade or so.

They were early enough to capture the prize table, set against the wall away from the noisy bonhomie of the long communal table where most of the Fellows were seated. Dick steered Marjorie into one of the four seats, then sat diagonally opposite her, making it clear to anyone who might consider joining them that the other two seats were off-limits.

"This had better be good." He nodded toward a florid figure at the long table, who had nodded a greeting and gestured for them to join the throng when they had entered the room. "The Bursar's got my number. Second time in a week I've been a naughty boy and sat in the corner. Not done, you know—especially not with a pretty lady."

"Flattery will get you everywhere, Dick. D'you think they suspect an illicit liaison?" She smiled and placed her hand on his, gazing with an expression of adoration up into his face. They had been lovers once, long ago in their student days, brought together by their common scientific interests. The common interests had outlasted the love affair, and they were now no more than friends and colleagues—but special friends, who went back a long way together. Unfortunately, as far as Marjorie's play-acting was concerned, everyone knew this. The last thing any of their acquaintances would suspect was an illicit liaison, no matter how much she held his hand and fluttered her eyelashes at him.

The arrival of soup stopped the game, for the time being. Dick paused until the waiter retreated, then started to steer the conversation round to what he presumed was the purpose of their meeting.

"How's Eve?"

"She's fine. Mixes well with the other chimps, but we don't leave them alone together, just in case. After all, she *is* different, and they might decide to gang up on her if no one was looking."

Marjorie's work with primates, mostly chimpanzees, had provided Richard with a ready-made home for his specimen. The papers still said Eve was a specimen of *Pan troglodytes*, and nobody seemed interested in arguing differently. One hairy chimp looks pretty much like another, and if Eve did stand out from the crowd it was only because she seemed a little more intelligent than the others, in spite of her relatively small head.

"That's good. I wouldn't want to have to go out there to find a replacement for her."

There was a silence while they both concentrated on eating. Marjorie was clearly building

herself up to ask something, and he certainly
owed her a favor for keeping Eve under wraps—
as if he wouldn't do anything he could for her
anyway. But she wasn't to be hurried. Desultory small talk, and an occasional acknowledgment of a greeting from someone passing their
table, occupied them through the main course.
Dick knew Marjorie would speak up when she
was ready; it came as she pushed back her plate
and chased a stray morsel from her lip with her
napkin.

"Eve's really important to your work, isn't
she?"

"Sure. She *is* my work, or she will be, once
I've dotted the *i*'s and crossed the *t*'s of the work
with Cobb."

"Nearly finished, then?"

"Yep. We know for sure that type twenty-
three works for diabetes, and we've just about
got the system for cystic fibrosis cracked. The
basic stuff'll be in the next issue of *J. Mol. Biol.*
There's more to come, of course. John's got
some ideas he wants to follow up, and he's got
this bright student to help him. But they don't
need me any more. The basic genetic research
is all done, and the techniques established. It's
going to be a production-line job soon, and I
want to stay with the blue-sky research."

"Because it's there."

He raised his glass in recognition of their private joke.

"Because it's there. Just for the hell of finding
out. And now I really can go my own way."

"The money?"

He nodded. "That and the prestige. The Bursar may not like my eating habits, but he knows

good publicity for the College, and curing disease is good publicity, even if he doesn't know how we've done it. The Institute's happy for me to stay and carry out my own research program. And there's the money. Thirty percent of the patent royalties on the basic technique, split between me and Cobb. One day, my child, you are going to have a very rich friend. Two rich friends, if you count Cobb."

"Fifteen percent doesn't sound too good."

"But ten percent of ten million is still a million."

"It's that big?"

"Sure it is. People have been dreaming of this since the 1970s. Not just identifying the parents at risk of producing babies with genetic disease, but actually doing something about it. Once Cobb's finished polishing it up for the production line, it'll be about as easy as visiting the dentist. The mother donates an egg cell, the clever doctor plucks out the dodgy gene and replaces it with a perfect one, using the tricks developed by yours truly, and it's fertilized in vitro. Once it's developing properly, bung it back in the womb and wait nine months for a healthy human baby."

"I believe you. But it won't work for diseases that aren't genetically inherited?"

She made the statement sound like a question. Richard realized that at last, in her own sweet way, Marjorie was getting around to the point of this meeting. Not before time, either, since the waiter was offering them dessert. He waved the pudding away, and Marjorie nodded assent.

"Just the coffee, thank you. Can you leave the pot?"

It wasn't really the done thing to treat the waiter, still called a college servant even in this day and age, like a human being. Richard always did. The waiter wasn't supposed to leave the whole pot of coffee with them on the side table. But he did. Older Fellows, like the Bursar, were capable of noticing both acts, and disapproving of them both, without ever linking cause and effect.

He poured the coffee. Black for her, with cream for him, no sugar.

"No, I'm a genetic engineer, not a magician. You guys out at the Center are going to be needed for a long time yet. Were you worried that I'd done you out of a job?"

Marjorie's work with primates centered on research into human diseases—hepatitis, leprosy, AIDS—diseases where the researchers had to have laboratory animals that were as much like *Homo sapiens* as possible.

"I wish you had. The way things are going, we're going to be out of business anyway before too long, *without* having achieved anything.

"D'you know what our biggest problem is?"

He shrugged, and sipped his coffee. The question was clearly rhetorical. She was going to tell him, whether he knew or not.

"We can't get enough chimps."

"You don't want me to go and get some, do you? That last visit to Africa was enough for me. Things are getting hairy down there."

"Of course not. Be serious. That's half the problem. Where we can get access, they've been practically wiped out. And where there are supposed to be breeding colonies, we can't get access because of the political situation."

And, Richard knew, chimps just didn't breed well in captivity. Nobody knew why, but things were getting worse. He had his own ideas on that. With only a few females ever producing infants, the need for animals was so desperate that the baby was taken from its mother as soon as possible, so that she would breed again. But that meant the infants were being reared in isolation, by people, and grew up neurotic and unable to cope with normal chimpanzee relationships, including sex. So in each generation the problem got worse.

"What's wrong with artificial insemination? Works well enough for cattle, after all."

"We've tried it. But chimps aren't cattle. The females bred in captivity mostly seem to be infertile, even with the benefit of artificial aids. The NIH, over in the States, is making a systematic study of the problem, but they're years away from a solution. Which is why I want your help. I want to go one better, and I want to do it before the NIH makes any progress. If you've got some spare time before you get on with your blue-sky research into human origins, I think we can do it together."

"If I can help, I will. But how?"

"You've worked on human genetic material, egg cells and so on, and human material is pretty much like chimp material, or there wouldn't be this crying need for more chimps."

"Hold on. If you're saying you expect me to find out why your lady chimps are infertile, and do something about it, well . . . "

"No, Dick. Listen. I want to try a *different* tack

from NIH, but I want to be sure you can work with chimp egg cells."

"Why not? I ought to be able to do anything with them that I can with the human kind."

"Great. So all we need is a host mother. They've done it with cattle, which is easy because they are members of the same species, and they did it with that mare, which was so surprised to give birth to a zebra. Let's do it with chimps."

At last, he caught her drift. It wasn't as easy as she seemed to think, but maybe it would be possible. It would certainly be an interesting challenge. Take a fertilized chimpanzee egg, and the egg from some other primate. After each one had begun to develop in the laboratory, strip out the central cell mass from the chimp egg, and wrap it up in the outer coat from the other egg, the developing blastocyst. Then if you could get the egg to implant successfully in the other mother's body . . .

He became aware of Marjorie's eager expression, and brought his eyes back into focus on her smiling face. Clearly, she knew she had him hooked, could tell that he was already planning how to set about the task. But he felt he ought to try to dampen her enthusiasm a little.

"It won't be easy."

"I know that, idiot. Just as long as it's possible."

"I can't set up a production line, you know. No way to turn out chimps by the dozen."

"Of course not. All I want is to prove the technique, then we can get people all over the world doing it. Let someone else work out the details

of mass production—like Cobb with your diabetes work."

"And we'll need a suitable surrogate mother."

"Don't worry about the host. I've got that end
all sorted out."

"In that case"—he admitted defeat—"I just
might be able to do it. For you. And"—he raised
his coffee cup—"because it's there."

Ten

For the next six months, Lee kept his work on Marjorie's project and his own research running in parallel. His side of the fertilization program turned out to be straightforward—simply borrowing techniques that had been applied successfully elsewhere, with other species, and adapting them to use with chimpanzees and other primates. In many ways, it was a logical extension of the work with Cobb, the main difference being that in those tests the eggs for fertilization had come from a human being, and were implanted back into that same human being after fertilization. But as far as he could tell they were getting nowhere, because of problems at Marjorie's end.

The chimps themselves seemed no more responsive to fertilization by this roundabout technique than to standard artificial insemination. Neither of them had thought they would be, but it was orderly and logical to try implanting an egg from one chimp into another chimp first, before looking to other species as hosts. But they hadn't had any better luck with using other primates as surrogate mothers, either. Large monkeys, even a gibbon, had all produced the same result, or lack of result. He could get the fertilized chimp egg, disguised in its blastocyst coat, dividing nicely in the lab. But it just wouldn't "take" when they tried implanting it in the host. Too much difference between the species? The other primates' natural defense mechanisms certainly seemed well able to spot the disguised chimpanzee egg cell, and reject it as foreign. There was probably some important clue to the workings of the immune system to be found there, but he wasn't inclined to follow up the lead. He'd do the best he could with the tools available, for Marjorie's sake, but his real interests lay elsewhere.

Richard kept the work ticking over, coaxing the separate components together to make new Trojan horses to try on other unsuspecting monkeys whenever Marjorie asked him, but privately he'd already given up on the project, and was concentrating almost entirely on his own work, now that the connection with Cobb and his team was officially severed and their last joint paper was about to appear in the *Journal of Genetic Biology*. They'd worked well together, and he owed Cobb a lot. But he could never fit in with a commercially oriented exercise like the one Cobb was now setting up, in collaboration with the Bluegene company, over in the science park.

Richard had never married—nobody seemed willing to put up with the hours he worked, and the clear fact that science came first in his life. Nobody except Marjorie, of course, but science came first in her life, too, which also left no scope for long-term commitments elsewhere. But he couldn't stand the cloistered college life, narcissistic and inward looking. And so he chose to live as far outside of town as was reasonably convenient, in a tiny two-bedroom house, one of a small square of cottages originally built as almshouses in the seventeenth century, and latterly refurbished, after a fashion, by a firm of property speculators. With the emphasis, as Dick never tired of telling his visitors, on the speculation rather than the property.

The phone rang just as he was leaving the small house in Bottisham. Cursing quietly, he shut the door and turned back. Wouldn't you know it—for once he was ready for an early start at the lab, and somebody had to call him up.

He picked up the receiver.

"Yeah?" He never answered with his name or the number. Let the caller make the first move. With any luck it would be a wrong number anyway. But his hopes were dashed.

"Dr. Lee?"

"Speaking." Might as well admit it, and get it over with.

"I'm calling from *This Week*, BBC-TV. We'd like to interview you about your theories concerning man and the apes."

"Uh, in what connection?"

"Well, we understand that you have a paper

coming out in *Nature* next week, and that it makes some rather startling claims about human origins."

"I wouldn't say startling. And in any case, I can't talk about that until it's published. The editor insisted."

"Of course not, Dr. Lee. We wouldn't broadcast the interview until the paper appears. But we would like to get it in the can before you talk to anyone else. And I do think that our viewers will be interested in the possibility . . ."—her voice changed, as she was clearly reading from a copy of his article—"that *Homo sapiens* and *Pan paniscus* are more closely related than the horse and donkey, and share a common ancestor not more than 3.2 million years ago."

He wondered if there was any way to put her off. The fundamentalists would have a field day with this. Church attendances were growing every year, and there was already trouble in Europe with the Cobb and Lee technique. "Against God's law," that crazy Frenchman had said. Interfering with nature—he seemed to think that innocent people should be allowed to have babies that would carry crippling diseases, when a simple bit of laboratory trickery could ensure that they were healthy. Richard could just imagine how that crowd would love the news that humankind wasn't very special at all, but biologically almost identical with the chimpanzees. Look what they did to Darwin. And *he* didn't even have molecular proof of the relationship. The better the evidence, Richard suspected, the worse the backlash was likely to be. He wondered if he'd dare use the comment

the Berkeley guys had made—"If God created
man, he created him in the image of an African
ape."

"Dr. Lee?"

Well, he couldn't just hang up on her. And the
BBC did still maintain certain standards, after
all. An idea which might keep some of the press
flack off him surfaced, and he acted on it at
once.

"I might be willing to give you an interview.
But I want a fee, and in return I'll make it an
exclusive. I'll guarantee not to talk to anyone
else, and you can syndicate the material to anyone who wants it. Okay?"

"I'll have to check with my producer, but it
sounds like a good proposal to me. When can
we talk to you?"

"I suppose you want to tape me at the lab."

There was a grunt of assent.

"Then there are a few formalities I'll have to
sort out. Call me there—do you have the number?"

Another grunt.

"Sometime after lunch, then, call me back and
we'll fix up the details."

They exchanged pleasantries, and he hung up.
He stood for a while in the small hallway, thinking. He didn't really want, or need, publicity at
this stage of the game. Plenty of time for that if
his plans succeeded fully. But he'd *had* to publish something, to establish priority.

There was plenty of time on the drive in to
the Institute to mull over the way he ought to
present his work to the media. He definitely
ought to stress the continuity of the work, ex-

tending back in an unbroken line for thirty-odd years to Sarich and Wilson in the sixties. Hell, he didn't want to be branded as the purveyor of revolutionary new ideas running counter to religious teaching, not in the present climate of opinion. After all, the old boys had nearly got it right when they said the proteins in the bodies of people and apes were so similar that they must have shared a common ancestor only five million years ago.

Of course, the paleontologists still didn't really believe it. Even when the DNA work in the seventies and eighties showed that human and chimp genes are exactly the same along ninety-nine percent of their length. Even now, some of them still held out for the human line being ten million years old, and few would come down below six million.

Richard moved the Renault out onto the roundabout where the village lane joined the main road, easing into the flow of traffic automatically, his thoughts completely preoccupied.

But he had to take some credit, after all. Had to make it clear his new work was a significant step forward, even if it did build on the work of others. Well, that shouldn't be too difficult. He could explain how it grew out of his work with Cobb, using the special enzymes to chop up bits of human genetic material and rearrange them. The old discovery of the six inversions, six bits of DNA that had got turned end for end, the mutations that made the difference between man and chimp. Old stuff that, from the seventies; then the new work, identifying precisely the length of each bit of inverted DNA, mapping out the genetic code letter by letter, with unprecedented precision, and dating the mutations. A kind of molecular archaeology.

He liked the phrase, and spoke it out loud, rolling it around his tongue. "Molecular archaeology." That should go down well on TV. Not rummaging around digging up bones of long-dead species, and hoping they might bear some relation to living people, but rummaging around with molecules from *living* animals, working out how they had got to be the way they are, and comparing one with another to see how they had evolved from a common ancestor.

Hell, I *know* my molecules have ancestors, he thought, but the fossil hunters can only *hope* their bones left descendants. Another good phrase. He rehearsed it mentally, practicing the half-smile he would use when he said it to the camera.

Yes, he had his presentation clear. Modest and unassuming, giving credit to his predecessors in a line of work going back a quarter of a century, and mentioning Cobb, but allowing the interviewer to draw out the fact that he alone, Richard Lee, had taken the final step which confirmed, beyond a shadow of a doubt, that mankind and the pygmy chimpanzee shared a common ancestor scarcely more than three million years in the past. And if the creationists didn't like it, they could bloody well lump it. Another few weeks' work, and he'd even be able to tell them which of the six inversions had occurred in the human line, and which ones took place in the chimp line, after the split.

He wondered, briefly, if he ought to let on that his work was actually slightly more specific.

That what he had actually proved, using DNA from blood samples, was that he, Richard Lee, and one particular pygmy chimp, Eve, shared a common ancestor no more than three million years in the past. After all, it was in the great scientific tradition, using yourself as the object of study. But he thought better of it. No need to encourage any questions about exactly what kind of chimp Eve was, and how exactly she had come to be resident in the primate center in Cambridge.

He swung off the northern bypass, onto the back road down through Madingley to the Institute. Quite a little science city they had down here now; the "new" Cavendish labs, getting on for thirty years old, the computing center, the old astronomy institute and the Royal Observatory buildings, and the Institute for Biomolecular Research, standing in its own grounds.

Richard slowed as he approached the gates. Hell's teeth. Another demonstration. A small group of mostly young people shouted incomprehensible slogans as he passed at walking pace under the first barrier, which dropped behind him, and stopped in front of the main gate to have his credentials checked. There were banners attached to the wire of the outer fence.

NATURES WAY IS THE BEST WAY
HUBRIS COMES BEFORE A FALL.

Might be more impressive, he told himself, if they knew some rules of punctuation. But deeper down he knew he was whistling in the dark. Those people might lack literary finesse, but they were getting more and more public

support. And it was the same across Europe.
Maybe he ought to emigrate to New Zealand.

He put on a bright smile for the guard. "More
entertainment for you today, then?" The gray-
haired man was not amused, taking his time
checking Richard's pass, not only comparing his
face with the picture on it but actually passing
the pass through the holo reader to test its va-
lidity.

"I can do without bloody entertainment like
that, Sir."

He handed the pass back and pushed the button to open the gate. Richard drove on. It's really going to make the security team's day, he
thought, when a BBC crew arrives with all their
gear. They're bound to want to shoot the demo
too, and that'll only encourage the crazies to act
up worse. This, he told himself firmly, is definitely not looking like one of the best days of
my life so far.

Eleven

"I've been set up." Richard reclined in the depths of the sofa, his long legs stretched out in front of him. A champagne glass, half empty, dangled in his right hand, from the arm resting on the side of the sofa. The perfect image of the TV screen hung on the opposite wall showed a man in clerical dress, talking earnestly to a young woman in a green suit.

"Come on, it's not that bad." Marjorie, sitting beside Richard, leaned forward to pick the champagne bottle off the low table, and then across him to top off his glass. She refilled her own, and carefully replaced the bottle on the table.

"Cheer up, Dick. You came across very well. Here's to success!" She raised the glass, and drank from it. He snorted, eyes fixed on the screen, and sipped at his own drink.

"Sure, what little they used came across all right. But they only used a couple of minutes of the interview, and now they're giving this servant of God all the time he wants to shoot me down. Just listen to him!"

She turned her attention to the screen. The interviewer was addressing her guest, who sat, nodding quietly, with his fingers steepled in front of his chest.

"Then how do you respond, Bishop, to the comment that if God did create man, He created man in the image of an African ape?"

The man smiled. "I see no difficulty with that at all. Of course, it is interesting to see what these scientific investigations reveal about the nature of people at a physical, molecular level. But neither they nor we can possibly pretend to know *why* God should have chosen a certain model, if I may use the word, as the basis for His design. The question you ask is, why should God have made man in the image of an ape? And my reply is simply, why not? The bodily form matters far less than the spirit, and whatever the similarities in the bodily form, I don't think even Dr. Lee would suggest that the African apes are the spiritual equivalent of ourselves.

"Indeed, this kind of discovery should, if anything, strengthen our Faith. It is all the more remarkable, and wonderful, that a bodily form so similar to that of a hairy chimpanzee should be able to carry within itself a human soul.

"I have no argument with Dr. Lee at all, nor with any scientists of his kind. As long as they are careful to deal only in physical and temporal matters, and leave spiritual affairs to those with the proper training in such matters."

"Thank you." The young woman turned to face the camera. "On that note, we have to end this discussion of the fascinating new insights into what it is that makes us human. Now it's back to David Fairclough for an update on the situation in the Middle East war. David—"

Richard, with another snort, stabbed at the remote control and silenced the TV, leaving the image of tanks rolling across the desert and antiaircraft missiles being fired flickering silently on the screen.

"Set up." He drained the glass, and held it out. "Fill 'er up, kid. Best piece of work I ever did, and the prattling prelate over there says it's just some amusing little kid's game, of no significance in the great cosmic plan. Stupid bugger."

Marjorie filled the glass and moved closer, putting her arm around him.

"It wasn't that bad, surely? He didn't attack you, just said your work was outside his province. Seems straightforward enough, even if you don't subscribe to his religion."

"Oh sure. Sweet bloody reasonableness on the screen, on the record. Wait and see what happens next, in the tabloids and out in the streets. We've already got a permanent demo running outside the lab. This stuff just encourages them. 'Why shouldn't God make man in the image of a chimpanzee?' " He mimicked the bishop's rounded, carefully paced tones. "Ye gods. Look at that lot." He gestured at the scenes of carnage on the screen. "And he says we're superior to the monkeys because of our unique soul. A chimpanzee'd have more sense than to get involved in that lot."

He brightened, momentarily, flashing a smile at Marjorie.

"That's it. My new project. I'll set up a program to prove that chimpanzees *have* got souls. Then we'll see what the smart-aleck bishop's got to say."

Subsiding back into a frown, he punched at the remote control again, flicking across the channels until he picked up a concert being broadcast live from Turin. But he left the sound off, with the orchestra blowing and scraping away for all it was worth in total silence.

"Dick." Marjorie was stroking his hair, absently. Slumped in the sofa, his head was below hers, resting on her shoulder. He could see her mouth and nose at the top of his line of vision, slightly out of focus, above and to his left.

"Dick."

"You said that."

"Look, this is rather bad timing, but there's something I wanted to talk to you about tonight. I thought it would be an ideal opportunity. You know, while you were flushed with triumph at the publicity. But it's all worked out wrong."

"Too late to take your champagne back. Terrible waste of two bottles of Bollinger."

"That's not important. Damn that bloody interview. I've been working myself up for this all week, but you're not going to be very receptive to my schemes in your present mood." She leaned over and kissed him, lightly, on the lips. To his surprise, he felt himself respond. His lips parted slightly and he lifted his head against

hers, feeling a familiar stirring in his groin. But
not so familiar in this context. What the hell's
going on? he thought. I haven't felt this way
about Marjorie in eight or nine years; and she
certainly hasn't shown any signs of feeling this
way about me. Must be the champagne. Is that
why she brought it over? Can't be. She said
she'd planned to discuss something, not to se-
duce me. What the hell. Make the most of it,
kid. At least the week won't be a total write-off.

He pushed himself more upright in the seat,
taking a more dominant role in the increasingly
enthusiastic kissing and caressing, until Marjorie pulled back, placing a finger on his lips.
Second thoughts? Well, if she'd changed her
mind he wouldn't press the issue. Their friend-
ship meant too much to him. But her eyes were
sparkling and she smiled at him.

"Don't you think we'd be more comfortable
upstairs? I think I can still find the way to the
bedroom, even if you've had too much to drink."

She stood, swaying slightly, and tugged at his
hand.

"You'll soon find out if I've had too much to
drink, young woman."

Standing up wasn't quite as easy as she made
it look, but the effort was obviously going to be
worthwhile. She led him by the hand up to the
bedroom, clearly in charge of the situation.
They left the lights off, with the curtains drawn
back and enough light coming in from the moon
for a not-so-surreptitious inspection of each
other as they undressed. Not bad at all, thought
Richard, for an old lady of thirty-six. The same
age, he told himself, as Marilyn Monroe was
when she died. Then, at last, his analytic facul-

ties gave up the unequal struggle with the effects of alcohol and hormones, and he had no more rational thoughts for a long time.

Sunlight and early birdsong woke him, much earlier than his usual Saturday-morning radio alarm. He opened his eyes to see Marjorie, wide awake, resting on one elbow, watching him.

"Hi." He smiled.

"Good morning, sleepyhead."

"What time is it?"

"Way past six."

He groaned, and made as if to pull the cover over his head. But she held it down, and poked him with a forefinger.

"You're getting fat, Dick. Successful middle-aged spread. More cuddly than you used to be."

He opened his eyes again, pretending to appraise her thoughtfully.

"You don't look so bad. Plenty of life left in you. Why did we leave it so long?"

"I had my reasons." She sat up, suddenly, hugging her knees and looking at him across the top of them, almost defensively, shielding her body from his direct gaze. "But that's an unfortunate choice of phrase. There's not so much life left in this body. After all, I'm thirty-six. The same age—"

"—as Marilyn Monroe was when she died." They laughed together.

"You remembered from my birthday?"

"As far as I can recall, that was my last conscious thought, last night."

"I'm flattered. At least, I think I'm flattered. You're certainly in a better mood now. Maybe

I ought to ask you my favor *before* cooking breakfast."

"Please, anything but that." Her cooking was a bad, and not at all private, joke. "I'll do anything you want, only let me cook my own breakfast."

"Anything, Dick?"

"Anything legal." Her expression became more serious, and he tried to lighten the tone again. "For you, anything nearly legal." Did she really have some illicit activity in mind?

She clearly came to a decision. It was time to get it off her chest. Now or never.

"It's partly to do with this aging body, Dick. There's something I want to do, and I won't be able to do it at all if I wait much longer.

"Basic biology. In a few more years, I'll be past child-bearing age." She looked at him steadily, straight in the eye, waiting for a reaction.

"Babies! *You* want babies!" Nothing could have surprised him more.

"And you want *me* to help?" A suspicion began to grow in his mind.

She fell back on the pillow, roaring with laughter.

"Oh, Dick, you should see your face! Don't worry, I haven't tricked you into anything you're going to regret in nine months' time. I'm not proposing marriage, and I'm not asking you to be the father of my child. Though, on reflection, I think I could do a lot worse." She sobered up again, but still lay there, looking up at him. "No, I just want some more help from you. And judging by the expression on your face, its going to seem easy compared with what's just been going through your mind. I *do* want to carry a baby, Dick; but I don't want you to be the father, and I'm not going to be the mother, either. It's simply a logical extension of the work you've already been doing for me . . ."

Twelve

There was no dramatic change in the situation outside the lab over the next few weeks. Instead, things gradually got worse, as the demonstrators gained in numbers and confidence, taking support from the publicity buildup following Richard's TV appearance. Engrossed in his new work with Marjorie, Richard scarcely noticed the steady escalation of hostility. Immediately after the broadcast, he'd been approached for interviews by other news media, and been tempted to take up the offers, in spite of his deal with BBC-TV, in order to hit back at his critics. But in the end he'd said no, referring inquiries to the full-length transcript of the original interview, including the part that had never been screened.

It didn't do him much good. In the subsequent coverage of the story, he appeared as a shadowy figure who had made outrageous claims about human ancestry, denying the role of God, and then retreated into his shell without offering any reply to the critics. It did indeed look as if he couldn't back up his claims. And that made him a natural target for all of the fringe groups who wanted, for whatever reasons, to close down research on human genetic material—an unholy alliance of religious fanatics and self-styled ecologists, plus the usual crazies who joined in any demonstration or confrontation with the establishment, and preferred it rough.

If it hadn't been for Marjorie's scheme, he might have noticed in time to do something about it—but what? Looking back in later months, it seemed to him as if there had been an inevitable progression of events, running away out of his, or anyone else's, control. Marjorie probably did him a good turn, by keeping him occupied and preventing him from getting involved in a fruitless, losing battle. At least, that's how he always rationalized things to himself later.

It wasn't that Marjorie's crazy scheme actually involved anything more difficult than the work he'd been doing already. If anything, it was easier. After all, he'd started out using Cobb's technique as applied to human ova, and adapted it to the chimps and monkeys. Taking the doctored chimp egg cell and getting it to implant into a human uterus was almost exactly the same as the work they had done with doctored human egg cells in the past. But the knowledge of what was involved, and *who* was involved, made him ultra cautious, double-checking at every step.

Marjorie was more sanguine. He had a strong suspicion that she'd planned this all along, anticipating, even hoping, that the work with primates would prove a dead end. He'd tried, at first, to change her mind, then suggested that they might get a younger, fitter volunteer. If she'd been planning to have a normal, human baby at her age, as a first-time mother she'd have been given extra care and attention, and kept in the hospital for the birth. "An elderly primogravida," that's what she'd be, in the jargon of the obstetrical trade. But she'd laughed his concern off.

"Look, Dick, first of all, I'm not absolutely sure that this is entirely legal."

"I'm absolutely sure it isn't. The Powell amendment is so vaguely worded that it can catch anything in its net."

"Okay, that just proves my point. So I can't put an advert in the *Cambridge Evening News*, asking for a healthy young girl to volunteer to be a surrogate mother to a chimpanzee.

"I know the risks to an old lady like myself with a first-time pregnancy, but you're forgetting something. This is going to be a chimp baby, and so it's going to be small, and it's going to have a gestation of just thirteen weeks. Probably nobody will even notice—I can always explain putting on a few pounds at my age. And we can both hole up in the country somewhere for the last month, then come back with a nice, new baby chimp. Nobody's going to think that's any more strange than when you came back from your field trip with a certain healthy specimen.''

He hadn't been sure if she'd actually meant to hint at a threat of blackmail; or simply to highlight the outstanding favor he owed her for providing Eve with board and lodging and no questions asked. But he had seen her determination, and, professing reluctance, agreed to go along with her scheme. Certainly, they had to keep everything under wraps until they'd proved the technique. Then they could publish the whole lot, chapter and verse, and let the experts worry about setting up a new legal framework to cope.

Just how reluctant had he really been? That was another question he would puzzle over for a long time, later. It *was* an exciting project, after all. If it worked, and they could sort out the legal complications, it would be the neatest way of solving the chimpanzee production problem imaginable. Hell, if it *were* legal, there were plenty of broody women who would, he was sure, jump at the chance. And it would be more likely to be interpreted as legal, even within the woolly requirements of the Powell amendment, if the world was presented with a *fait accompli*. He'd seen—was seeing—the power of the media. Marjorie, cooing over a cuddly little chimp, ought to be a human-interest story that would work.

It would also, he admitted to himself, be satisfying to rub the noses of the NIH team in the dirt. Serve them right, for trying to be too damned clever, and not using nature's way. What it all boiled down to, the ultimate reason for doing any piece of research, was the old one of their habitual toast. They hadn't actually discussed it in those terms, and neither had used the toast since the decision to proceed had been made. That, in itself, was an unspoken agreement between them. He knew that she knew, and she knew, he was sure, that he knew. The real reason for doing it was for the hell of it—because it was there to be done.

The actual implantation was routine. Since Bob Edwards and Patrick Steptoe had pioneered the test-tube baby technique (like most scientists, Richard hated the term, but accepted that it had become part of the language) almost any competent physician, or a biologist with the appropriate training, could do the trick, either with a fresh fertilized ovum or one thawed out from stock. Not that thawing one out from stock was legal, of course, for fertilized human egg cells. Which was one of the gray areas where he and Marjorie could, if things went wrong, get caught by the Powell amendment. After all, the chimp DNA was encased in a human blastocyst (derived, of course, from one of Marjorie's ova).

He'd also checked in the library on the laws of inheritance. Amusingly, and as he'd suspected, the law took great pains to set out how paternity might be established, but hadn't caught up with the times as far as maternity went. Marjorie would, in law, indeed be the mother of the baby that would issue, in due course, from her womb (he liked the word "issue." It had a nice legalistic ring to it). That ought to set a few legal pigeons fluttering, when they finally broke the news to the world at large.

But that was all in the future, more Marjorie's concern than his.

Or was it? They hadn't made love since that night three weeks ago. They wanted no interference with the experiment, and both of them had fallen naturally into their scientific roles, treating Marjorie's reproductive apparatus as simply an integral part of that experiment, to be poked and prodded at as necessary, but only with sterilized instruments. And yet, they'd been spending a lot of time together, and it felt very comfortable. Occasionally, when not absorbed in his work, Richard began to wonder if life might not be more comfortable all round with someone to share things with. And if he was going to share his life with anybody, it would certainly be Marjorie.

It was in this vaguely optimistic, happy frame of mind that Richard swung the Renault round the sweeping left turn into the approach to the Institute. Relaxed, driving on autopilot, he scarcely had time to notice the extent of the crowd outside the gates before he was upon them, braking sharply to avoid hitting a young girl who ran, screaming, into his path and hurled herself on the hood of his car.

From the corner of his eye, he noticed a green truck parked just off the road, and a camera crew running across the grass. Bastards! he thought. Playing up for the cameras. And if the sodding cameramen would only keep away . . .

He stopped thinking, and began to concentrate on self-preservation. Fists were hammering on the roof and sides of the car, with faces pressed up against the glass. Someone had

opened a can of red paint, and threw it, most
going over the bodies plastered against the car,
but a little going on the driver's door and window. Thank God the doors were locked. Since
the crowds had started getting bigger, he'd
taken to locking up all round from inside the
car, using the safety feature designed to stop
children opening doors on the road.

He began to inch the vehicle forward, through
the press of bodies, and as a gap opened up he
saw uniformed figures, with dogs, running from
the opened gates. About time, too. Where the
hell had they been? Having a tea break? The
crowd parted, having vented itself for the benefit of the media, and unwilling to provoke the
guards into releasing the dogs they held, bark-
ing, on short chains. Richard sighed with relief
and accelerated, changing up into second gear.
At that moment, from ahead and to his left, a
brick came hurtling out of the mob, smashing
into the windshield and coming through into the
passenger seat. His vision suddenly obscured by
the shattered glass in front of him, Richard
eased off on his right foot, but held the car
straight and kept moving, trusting to luck to get
through the gates, and trusting the guards' instinct for self-preservation to get them out of
his way. The pillar of the second barrier passed
by his red-spattered window, he slammed his
foot on the brake and stopped, breathing heav-
ily.

A face appeared, and a hand tapping on the
window.

"Are you all right, sir?"

It was Joe, the eternal optimist, the Institute's very own little ray of sunshine. I bet

he's enjoying this, thought Richard. But he put on his best smile as he pressed the button to unlock the doors and wind all the windows down.

"Never felt better, Joe. Do you want to check my pass?"

The Director, very decently, gave Richard time to clean up and have coffee before summoning him into his office. He turned off the screen set in his desk as Richard came into the room.

"Dick! That must have really shaken you up. Come in, sit down. Can I get you some coffee?"

"I've just had one, thanks."

"Ah, yes. Something stronger, perhaps? In the circumstances? Brandy?"

Richard shook his head. Oh Christ, he thought. Calling me Dick *and* offering me brandy. I'm up shit creek without a paddle.

He sank back in the proferred seat, and waited while the Director arranged some papers on his desk, and settled himself down.

"Dick, I'm afraid the activities of those people out there"—he gestured at the window, ignoring the fact that it opened out onto green fields, with no sign of the gates or the demonstrators—"are beginning to pose something of a problem."

"I'd noticed."

"Yes, well." The Director shuffled the papers again. "The fact is, even before this morning's little incident, I've been under pressure. From London."

"Serc?"

The Science and Engineering Research Council held the purse strings of the Institute, and was the only body in London, or anywhere else for that matter, that the Director took much notice of.

"Directly, yes. And indirectly, shall we say, sources close to Number Ten."

The Prime Minister? Richard's capacity for mind-boggling, strictly limited, began to overload. What did the Prime Minister care about his comparative study of chimp and human DNA? Surely he couldn't have got wind of anything else?

Taking Richard's silence as understanding acquiescence, the Director continued.

"The fact is, Dick, this is a tricky time all round. Our budget comes up for review next year, and the election is due the year after. As things stand, we're doing quite well. Not as well as I'd wish, but the Minister for Science is sympathetic, and I think most people would say we've been getting our share of funds." He smiled, the smile he used to ingratiate himself with committees. "Some might say we've been getting more than our share." Having waited, unavailingly, for Richard to laugh, he continued.

"Now, I don't know how much notice you pay to these things. I understand you've been rather wrapped up in your work lately. But there does seem to be a groundswell of public opinion that's rather taken against our kind of work in general, but more specifically against your own work. Some wild talk. You know the sort of thing. Government money being used to encourage anti-Christian activities. Nonsense, but damaging nonsense if it doesn't die down by election time. And, of course, the election could come sooner than some people think."

He stood up, and paced over to the window, standing with his arms folded behind his back, gazing outward, as if too embarrassed to face Richard.

"Of course, it's all nonsense. Probably die down in a few months. But as things stand, the people in London think it might be a good idea if you took an indefinite leave of absence. Stay away from the lab. A sabbatical, if you like." He turned around. "In the States, perhaps?"

"You mean, as far away from here as possible?"

The Director spread his hands, in a gesture of helpless resignation, as if to say, it's nothing to do with me, chum, I'm just following orders.

"What about Cobb?"

"There doesn't seem to be quite so much bad feeling about John. He hasn't, after all, been sounding off on TV. And, of course, he's scarcely in here these days, what with his work at Bluegene . . ."

A light dawned on Richard.

"You mean, *one* of us has to be given to the wolves, and since I'm not the one who's bringing a fat contract from industry into the Institute, I get the short straw."

"Not quite the way I'd put it, Dick, but yes. For the good of the rest of us. And only on a temporary basis, I assure you." He nodded at the screen. "You've already been on TV again, this morning. A newsflash on Six. I really do think it would be best if we could resolve this thing quickly."

"I'll think about it. But don't go changing the locks on my door yet. Give me a day or two."

"Of course, Dick."

"I can always spend a couple of terms holed up in College, and write a book about this stuff."

The Director frowned. "I hope that's a joke, Dick. If so, it's in very poor taste." He pressed a button and the door opened. His secretary stood there, ready for orders.

"Sir?"

"Dr. Lee will be taking the rest of the day off, Carol. The police should be here"—he glanced at the old-fashioned watch he wore on his left wrist—"in about five minutes, to see there's no trouble outside." He turned to Richard, "I took the liberty, Dick. Assumed you wouldn't want to drive your car in that condition. Leave it here as long as you like. And I'll be hearing from you tomorrow?"

Richard grunted something that might have been an affirmative, rose, and followed Carol out of the room. Bad taste, eh? Why not. A bestseller to really embarrass the bastards. It'd knock spots off old Jim Watson's *Double Helix*. Hell, he was finished here. Marjorie's pregnancy seemed to have taken, all they had to do was let nature take its course. Three goddamn marvelous bits of work—with Cobb, the evolu-

tion stuff, now Marjorie. And all the thanks he
got was being chucked out on his ear to appease
the mob. Might as well be in Ancient Rome as
in Cambridge. Only there it had been the Christians thrown to the lions, not the scientists
thrown to the Christians.

Thirteen

He asked the sergeant to drop him off at the College, and strode out across the lawn toward the square, white building set along the river. Inside his room on the first floor, he closed the heavy door with a sigh of relief. The right-hand drawer of the old, leather-topped desk proved rewarding. A half-bottle of scotch, scarcely touched. He picked out the least smeared of the assortment of glasses in the cupboard, and decided that anything that could live in neat whisky was welcome to live in his stomach. Pouring himself a generous measure, he walked over to the window, opened it, and sat on the long couch beneath, feet up, listening to the birdsong.

He needed another month or so in a decent molecular biology lab to sort out his work on the inversions in the human and chimp chro-

mosomes. Once he published that, he'd be a free
agent, with no work in progress and no ties.
With his experience, he'd easily get a post
somewhere. Wouldn't he?

But where to finish the job? He'd no intention
of going cap in hand to Cobb and asking for a
loan of the Bluegene facilities, though he was
sure such a request would be granted. There
were no facilities of the kind he needed at the
primate center. London? He dismissed the
thought. Richard hated London, and didn't really have any good contacts there. Norwich.
Now, *that* was a good idea. He had good contacts there; MacRobyn, the climatologist he'd
met on the working group looking into destruction of tropical habitat. That would do nicely.
He could even commute to Norwich, it was only
about fifty miles from Bottisham, straight down
the A11.

By the time the glass was empty, he felt a lot
better about the way things were going. Carefully shutting the whisky away in the desk, for
future need, he set out again across the sunlit
lawns to the Bursar's office. The door, as always, was open. No problem getting into the
outer office; the inner sanctum might be a different story.

"Hello, Mary."

The middle-aged woman seated at the word
processor smiled in acknowledgment of his
greeting.

"You've been in the wars, I hear, Dr. Lee. I'm
glad to see you're not hurt."

He winced. "News travels fast. Mind if I make
a phone call? Only local; I always call my bookie
in Los Angeles from the Institute." He picked

up the phone as he spoke, taking her assent for granted. "And if the Bursar's free after lunch, maybe you could book me in for a chat. You might be seeing more of me around here than you expected."

He'd been punching numbers as he spoke, and as Mary started to reply he held up his hand, not registering the sudden disappearance of the smile from her face. Only the one word "Actually . . ." passed her lips, then she shrugged and returned to her typing while he got on with the call.

"Dr. Cooper, please."

"Marjorie? Dick. Hi. I'm glad I caught you. You haven't been watching TV, have you?"

She hadn't.

"Okay. Well, I'm in the news again. Nothing to worry about." That was as much for the benefit of Mary and the Bursar. "I just wanted to let you know I'm fine, and you're not to believe any rumors you hear."

She denied ever listening to rumors.

"No problem, then. Dinner tonight? About eight? Okay, see you then. Take care."

He set the handset down and turned his attention back to Mary.

"Sorry, Mary. You were saying?"

"Actually, Dr. Lee, when you've finished using my phone to make a date, the Bursar was hoping you'd call in. He said he could see you any time. I think that includes now. Shall I tell him you are here?"

He nodded. News *did* travel fast.

Mary thumbed a button on her console. "Dr. Lee is here, Bursar. Will you see him now?"

The machine squawked unintelligibly. She released the button, and nodded at Richard. "He's all yours."

The Bursar's study could have come, apart from the electric light and the communications console on the desk, straight out of the nine-teenth century. Ancient books lined the walls; a crystal decanter filled with, Richard knew, rather better sherry than he kept in his own room, stood with sparkling glasses on a side ta-ble near the window. The two leather arm-chairs looked as if they came from a Victorian gentleman's club—in fact, they probably did. .

"Good of you to come by, Dick. Sherry?"

He was already pouring. It was hard to turn down the Bursar's offer of a drink, whether it was sherry before lunch or port after dinner. Oh well. It'll probably mix well with the whisky.

"Thank you. Just a small one." A useless plea. The Bursar only poured in one size—large.

His task completed, the Bursar handed over one glass to Richard and raised the other to his lips, sipping appreciatively.

"Well, let's not stand on ceremony." He waved his visitor into one of the comfortable chairs, settling his own bulk in the other.

"I understand there've been some problems at the Institute. Nasty business." He shook his head. "Just as well nothing like that ever hap-pens around here."

The first, faint ringing of warning bells sounded far away in the back of Richard's mind.

It was raining again when Richard left the of-fice. The same light, warm rain that seemed to have been falling for most of the so-called summer. He scarcely noticed, but automatically stuck to the path instead of crossing the increasingly damp lawn. He was still stunned by the Bursar's polite, but firm, insistence that Richard's future as a Fellow of the College depended upon an assurance that he would "not pursue" the line of work that had recently brought so much adverse publicity down upon him. In vain, he'd tried to protest that the whole point of a scientific fellowship, such as the one he held, was to provide freedom to do any kind of research—freedom that Cambridge was supposed to hold dear, and guard jealously against outside interference. The Master, it seemed, had already spoken to the Bursar, who was, in effect, simply the appointed hatchet man. And who was pulling the Master's strings? Serc or Number Ten? Either way, the message was quite clear. If Dr. Richard Lee was going to keep rocking the boat, then the review of his fellowship due at the end of the next term, which ought to have been a formality, would find him no longer a fit person to hold an honored position in this College. And other colleges were, it was suggested, likely to feel the same way.

It was crazy. They were just running scared. Oh, he could see some of the reasoning behind their arguments. Scenes like the one at the Institute this morning wouldn't go down too well among the hallowed cloisters of the old colleges in the heart of town. Bad for the tourist trade. Might disturb the dust of centuries on the walls. But surely they could see that this would all blow over in a week or two? It was only a minority protest—admittedly a vociferous minority. There was more going on behind the scenes.

Political pressure. The Master—the bloody
Master had been a politician himself, until he
retired at the last election. Jobs for the boys, a
nice little sinecure as notional head of a Cambridge college, big house, prestige—and someone on the spot to keep the more maverick
academics in line. Yes, if Number Ten said
"frog" the Master would jump, as high as they
wanted.

Richard shook his head, muttering to himself
as he worked it all out. This bloody country was
going to the dogs. More restrictions and in-
fringements of the traditional liberties every
year. Government that didn't care about science, and looked with suspicion on all academics. Cutbacks in education, so most young
people never had a chance to find out that they
were being oppressed. Sure, it was more subtle
than tanks on street corners and military juntas
in power. But just as effective. And they'd win
the next election, for sure. After all, Hitler had
come to power legally, in a democratic election.
New Zealand, he thought, here I come.

But his absorbed, brisk march through the
rain-spattered streets had brought him, not to
New Zealand, but to the garage which regularly
serviced his car. He pushed through the swing
door, only realizing how damp he was when the
warm, dry air hit his face, and walked over to
the reception desk.

The young man behind the console recog-
nized him, though Richard couldn't recall seeing him before.

"Good afternoon, Dr. Lee. What can we do for
you?"

"I've left my car at the Institute, out on Mad-ingley Road, with a broken windshield."

The youth smiled. "Sure, we saw it on the news, just now."

"There may be some other damage, too. I'd like someone to collect the car and get it fixed."

"No problem. Do you want it delivered to your home, or will you collect?" His fingers were flying over the keyboard as he spoke, set-ting up the job.

"Collect. I'll need to hire one of your cars un-til it's fixed, and I'll drop that off at the same time."

"Okay." He tapped at the keys again. "If you want something now this minute, we've only got the old Metro, or there's a 35 XL, but that's more expensive."

The old Metro was a clunker, the emergency "spare vehicle" that the garage had had on the books for ten years. It was beat up, and had some enormous mileage on the clock, but it was regularly maintained and ran well. Richard had used it twice before.

"As long as it's still got a wheel at each cor-ner, the Metro will do fine." He handed over his card, and the receptionist ran it through the machine, watching the screen. He frowned, then tried again. Embarrassed, he turned his atten-tion back to Richard.

"I'm sorry, Dr. Lee, but there's a problem. You've been reclassified as an unacceptable in-surance risk."

"But that's ridiculous! I haven't been running down little old ladies! It must be some mis-take—try again."

"Uh, no, Dr. Lee. There isn't any problem

about your record as a driver. But the insurers seem to think that any car you're driving might become a target—like this morning. I'm sorry, there's nothing I can do. We have to go by the book."

"But that was just an isolated incident. And it was only a couple of hours ago . . ." His voice trailed off.

"If it's been on TV, Dr. Lee, you can be sure they picked it up. Doesn't take long for the computer to make the correlations. It's only listed as a temporary restriction. Maybe they'll lift it soon."

"But that's crazy. I have to have a car. There's no angry mob here threatening to wreck it the moment I sign the papers."

"Dr. Lee, I really can't help. But I'll call the manager, if you like."

Richard nodded, and the young man typed a brief message on the console.

"He'll be right with you."

Richard tried to control his fury. He wanted to smash the place apart, kick in the screen of the computer, but he knew it would only make things worse. Be reasonable, he told himself. Be pleasant, be polite. He repeated it, like a mantra. They're only doing a job. Charm them round to your side. And as he consciously took a few deep breaths, trying to act with logic instead of emotion, a possible solution came to him.

The manager clearly expected trouble. He glanced nervously from side to side, and steered Richard away from the main desk, where three other customers were pretending not to be fascinated by the altercation.

"Dr. Lee. You are one of our most valued customers . . ."

"It's quite all right. I appreciate that you have no influence over the insurers."

The manager's relief at Richard's quiet, reasonable tone was apparent. Good, thought Richard. Right tactics. Be calm, be reasonable.

He pulled out his checkbook. "I only want to hire your old Metro for a couple of days. It isn't exactly the pride of your showroom, and it can't be worth more than a few hundred pounds."

"Well, yes." The manager swallowed, trying to see what Richard was getting at.

"So, suppose I give you my check for, shall we say, one thousand pounds. I take the Metro, and when I bring it back we can tear up the check. Or, if anything happens to the vehicle while it's in my possession, well, it becomes my problem, not yours."

The manager held the check in this hand. "That does sound acceptable, Dr. Lee. And, of course, your own personal insurance policy covers you to drive other vehicles?"

"Of course."

He nodded assent. "Wait here." He walked over to another console at the back of the room, typed briefly at the keyboard, then came back to Richard. "The car will be out front by the time you get there, Dr. Lee. I've entered it as a courtesy loan, free of charge, while your vehicle is being repaired. The least I can do. We value your custom, and we hope you'll keep coming back to us for many more years."

"Thank you," Richard maintained a calm exterior, but raged inwardly.

"Courtesy car" meant no paperwork, no

comebacks for the manager if anything went wrong. If the car wasn't *officially* rented to him, nobody could accuse the manager of going against the instructions in the computer. So much for being a "valued customer." Smarmy little bootlicker, he thought. But so am I. And it worked. The soft answer turneth away wrath, and getteth one a set of wheels for the week.

Fourteen

Marjorie swirled the last of her brandy round in the glass, holding it so that the light from the candle shone through the liquid. They'd eaten well—Richard's cooking, at home. She had hardly drunk anything, one glass of wine and the half-finished brandy, in deference to her "delicate condition," as Dick mockingly referred to it. Richard, however, had finished off most of the bottle of claret on his own. And he'd filled her in on the events of the day.

He finished his own brandy, and set the empty glass down beside his coffee cup. The dishes, stacked in the machine in the kitchen, could wait for morning. "I'd hardly got in this afternoon when I had Euronet calling, from Bonn. Apparently this is an international story, now. They sounded very sympathetic. Said they wanted to do a piece about freedom of speech, and of research, rights of the individual, all that stuff. Someone must have tipped them off about the political pressure, as well as the riot." He half smiled. "Coming to something, kid, when the Germans have to instruct us in the rights of the individual and freedom of speech."

"What did you say?"

"Oh, nothing much. Gave them the brushoff, really. After the way the beeb screwed me around, who needs it?"

"I don't know, Dick. Maybe you could use some good publicity just now."

"Who's to say if it will be good or bad? Even if Euronet is unbiased, you'll only get bits taken out of context and replayed on the local news over here. No, leave it all alone. I tell you, if I had a castle I'd just pull up the drawbridge and stay inside until all this blows over."

"What about me?"

"With you inside, of course."

"Be careful, If that's a proposal, I just might accept it." She poured some more coffee for herself, but set the pot down when he shook his head to indicate that he had had enough. Was she joking about sharing his castle? Was he joking when he made the offer? Richard was just fuddled enough by the wine and brandy to be slightly uncertain of his next move. He wondered if he ought to pursue the theme, but she forestalled him.

"So, what next?"

"Now this minute, or in life in general?"

"Both."

"Well, in general, I'm through with the Institute. I think the guys in Norwich will play ball. I phoned MacRobyn when I got in—"

"MacRobyn?"

"Yeah, the climatologist. I know him from the ecology of the tropical rain forest study—you know, the EEC thing I worked on a couple of years back."

She nodded. The Common Market, in its attempts to be taken credibly as a molder of world opinion, had latched on to the environmental crisis and put a major effort into research on the tropical environment. Some of the studies suggested that the destruction of the tropical forest was contributing to the funny weather lately. In a big research project run by the European bureaucracy. there had been plenty of scope for a few smaller, pet schemes to squeeze under the financial umbrella, including some studies of the effects of forest clearance on other species, like Richard's favorite chimps.

"Well, Mac's a good guy, a bit of a maverick himself. Probably the Celtic blood—he's Manx, and proud of it. Claims to have Viking ancestors, and tells you that the Isle of Man has the oldest parliamentary democracy in the world.

"Anyway, he's setting up a meeting tomorrow with the molecular biologists and somebody in administration. He thinks he can pull a few strings and get me a temporary home up there, to finish the evolution stuff. No money, but I don't need any for a few months, at least. Then I publish the results with grateful thanks to the University of East Anglia, and they use my fame to recruit hordes of eager scientists. Or something."

"Can I come along for the ride?"

"Tomorrow? Sure. Why not. I'm going to go in to the Institute first thing, early, and clear up my desk. But it'd be nice to have you along."

"Which"—she smiled—"rather sorts out the problem of the immediate future, doesn't it?"

He grinned back, "I was hoping you'd stay."

"But"—she wagged a forefinger with mock solemnity—"no hanky-panky. I don't want to shake up that little experiment we've got running inside me. Strictly chaste cuddles for the time being."

"Chaste?"

"Well, cuddles, anyway . . ."

He took her hand, and they went off to bed.

Even at eight o'clock the next morning, there was a small knot of demonstrators outside the gate to the Institute. But there was also a police car, prominently parked just off the road, the bright orange and red stripe down its side a reassuring sight to Richard. One policeman, his cap pulled down over his eyes, appeared to be asleep in the driver's seat. Another was chatting to the security guard. Nobody took much notice of the nondescript blue Metro, until Richard pulled up at the barrier and proffered his pass. Then, a quick wave of recognition ran through the demonstrators.

"Hey, it's him, quick—"

But before they could take any action, the car was through the barrier, with a nod from Richard to the police constable. In the rearview mirror, he noticed the other policeman, not asleep

after all, sitting up and talking into a microphone. One of the scruffier demonstrators
seemed to be writing something down in a notebook, the rest were going through a halfhearted
chorus of ritualistic chants.

"Well, here we are. I'm actually beginning to
feel glad to be shut of the place."

Marjorie said nothing.

Inside the building, two cleaning ladies were
finishing a cup of tea in the small kitchen before going home. The night guard was still on
at the front door, a young man that Richard
didn't know by name, and there was the hum of
a photocopying machine at work in the Director's secretary's office. Otherwise, the place
seemed to be deserted.

"Lab first, then desk."

Again Marjorie didn't reply, but tucked her
arm through his, lending moral support. He felt
a warm, protective glow. He'd definitely had
enough of being a loner.

There was actually very little clearing up to
be done in the lab. A few samples, blood serum
from himself and from Eve, he took from the
fridge and packed carefully in an insulated box,
the little glass bottles nestling in their padded
pockets inside. He could always get more, but
it seemed best to get this stuff over to Norwich
at once, as a precaution. Other bottles were
washed out, and placed in the sterilizer.

The printed records took a little more time.
Richard wasn't worried about the listings of his
own official work, printed out and kept, as a
matter of routine, until the data were analyzed
and results published. Technically, that all belonged to the Institute—ultimately, to Serc.

Marjorie's stuff, though—well, everyone knew
he'd been doing something for her, and it might
look odd if he seemed to be trying to cover it
up.

"What do you think, kid? Shall I burn this lot,
or leave it?"

"What does it say, exactly?"

"Well, it's got details of all the cross-
fertilization work. Donors, hosts, all the usual
stuff. But there's nothing here to identify the
animals, except a code reference. If I remove
this page"—he did so, dropping it in his case—
"then nobody here can identify which animal
from the primate center is a host and which one
is a donor in any of the tests."

"I assume you include me in the category of
experimental animal."

"Of course." He put his arm round her and
kissed her. "And I've got some more experiments planned, in the fullness of time."

"In that case, leave the rest of it. The obvious
place to keep the details of the animals is at the
primate center, and if anyone asks I'll give them
something, suitably doctored.

"It's nice to know that you think of me as experimental primate number forty-seven."

"Don't exaggerate." He pretended to consult
the list. "You're only number twenty-three in
my little black book. And you aren't an experimental primate. Only donors get that status.
You're merely a host mother."

She put out her tongue at him.

"What next?"

"That's it, here. If they're chucking me out,
the least they can do is clean up after me." He
gestured at the clutter in the lab. "I'd give my

eyeteeth for some of this equipment, though. You know, for fifty kay you could fit out a pretty neat private lab."

"What you need is a sponsor."

"Yeah, or a pools win. Then I could be an independent scientist, do my own work, and to hell with the scientific establishment, universities, and Serc."

"Jim Lovelock did it. I read about him in *New Scientist* when I was a teenager. 'Britain's independent FRS.' Had his own lab in Devon, and made a living out of it, inventing environmental sniffers to trace pollution."

"But I'm not Lovelock. And that was twenty years ago. Things have changed since the seventies. Nobody's gonna buy inventions from a lone wolf today. Cobb's got the right idea—set up with a tame company."

They'd been walking while they talked, the coolbox swinging from Richard's right hand, Marjorie carrying his case.

"Well, here we are." They stopped outside the door of his office. "Six years of my life. Coming to an end." He leaned on the door, but it refused to open. Frowning, he set the coolbox down and fumbled in his pocket for his keys. The Yale had hardly ever been used, in all his time at the Institute, but he'd stuck it on the key ring on his first day there, and it had been with him ever since.

"Who's been locking my door?"

Inside, everything was in order. Marjorie turned the lights on, and Richard sat at the desk, pulling open drawers and dumping their contents into an empty computer-paper box that he'd taken from the bookshelf.

"I'll get someone to bring the books over to my place later. They should be glad to, to see the back of me."

He found half a bar of plain chocolate at the back of a drawer, broke off a piece and put it in his mouth.

"Want some?" he mumbled, holding it out to Marjorie. She shook her head. A coffee mug emblazoned with a white horse on a maroon background, and the legend "Kent CCC" went in the box. A couple of old pens, paperclips, and a handful of assorted junk went into the round metal wastepaper basket, with a clatter.

"Feeling strong?"

She shook her head. "I'll take the coolbox, you bring the heavy stuff."

"I suppose you're going to plead mitigating circumstances." He grunted as he hefted the box up on to the desk. "Heavier than it looks. I'll get one of the security guys to give us a hand."

But before he could reach the door, there was a knock. Richard raised his eyebrows, looking quizzically at Marjorie, and said, "Yeah?"

The door opened, and the Director of the Institute came into the small room. "Dick, how nice." His eyes flicked around, taking in the evidence of packing. "And Dr. Cooper, isn't it?" He held out his hand to Marjorie, who shook it perfunctorily.

"I see you've taken my advice to heart, Dick. Well done. A year away, let the fuss die down, and we'll be glad to have you back."

"Maybe. I've got to write up my latest work." He didn't feel it wise to mention the need for more lab studies. "That'll take a few weeks. After that, my plans aren't clear."

"But you're not planning to write that book, hmm? Just a little joke?"

Richard glanced at Marjorie. "Just a little joke. Dr. Cooper, here, talked me out of it."

"I *am* glad." The Director positively beamed at Marjorie. "And how is your own work going?"

"So so. We really need more animals, but it's a hell of a job getting them out of Africa now."

"Ah, yes." The Director clearly had no real interest in other people's problems. He looked, pointedly, at his watch.

"Well, Dick, this is all very splendid. Can I take it you will be leaving the premises today?"

"There's the books—"

"Oh, I'll get someone to drop them over for you. No trouble. You see, I'd rather like to make an announcement to the press. That your work here is completed, you're taking a sabbatical, recharging the batteries—you know the sort of thing."

"Get the mob off your back, huh?"

The Director frowned. "You do have an unfortunate way of putting things. But the timing could be just right. I have it on good authority"—he lowered his voice, though there was nobody around to hear—"that the government plans to introduce legislation. An early-day motion, being put down by a backbencher, but they are going to give it their support."

"What kind of legislation?"

"Oh, nothing too draconian. New guidelines for research on human genetic material. Restrictions on applications—licenses, that sort of thing."

"Actually, Dick"—for a moment Richard thought that he was going to be physically patted on the back—"actually, I think you'll do rather well out of it. All the existing material, stuff with patents applied for and so forth, will be allowed to stand. Bluegene and your friend Cobb will stay in business, especially the export business, and you'll get your share of the royalties. But I don't think there'll be any new work going on along these lines, not here, at any rate."

"So I get thrown to the wolves. Bluegene gets a monopoly, the Government is seen to be taking action, and after they win the next election the Institute gets an increased budget. Right?"

The Director ignored his outburst.

"There'll always be a place for you here, Dick, once the fuss has died down."

"You're crazy. Can't you see it's the thin end of the wedge? Let these lunatics win this time, and they'll be back, with more and more restrictions. There won't *be* an Institute to come back to, before long!"

"Dick." Marjorie's quiet voice stopped the tirade. "There isn't any point in arguing. You're leaving anyway, aren't you?"

"Yeah. Okay." He picked up the coolbox and headed for the door. "You don't mind if I get someone to bring the box out to the car?"

"Of course not, Dick. This is all just a storm in a teacup. I know you've been under stress. The rest will do you good."

Richard strode down the corridor, Marjorie half breaking into a run to keep up with him.

"Bastard. Can't you hear him. By teatime he'll have convinced himself that I'm suffering from a nervous breakdown, and that he's been kind to me.

"Oh, sod the lot of them."

Fifteen

He felt better almost as soon as they were on the road. The weather seemed to have relented, for a change, and he drove with the window half open. Marjorie, beside him, fiddled with the radio for a few minutes, trying to find something interesting, then gave up. The coolbox nestled on the seat behind them. What more did he want? His career, so far, had followed its own inexorable momentum, from school to university, to research, to postdoctoral work. At every stage there was one more logical hurdle to be jumped, one more step to take up the ladder. He'd never really planned anything, it just happened. But now? He really was his own man, now. He could probably tough it out for a year or two—sell the house if need be—maybe move in with Marjorie. He glanced across at her and smiled.

She smiled back. "Feeling better?"

"Yeah. Thinking."

"Okay."

She closed her eyes, and leaned back in the seat, happy to leave him to his thoughts, if that was what he wanted.

And then—the picture was unfolding neatly in his mind—in two years, max, the money from Bluegene would start rolling in. He wouldn't be stinking rich, but if he was careful he'd never have to work again in his life, if he didn't want to. And if he *did* want to, there had to be somewhere he could get a modest post. Even Norwich.

They were passing the Science Park, some of the trees already beginning to show their autumn colors.

"Hey, look at that."

Marjorie opened her eyes. He slowed the car, and they took in the array of golds and purples splashed amongst the greenery. The weak sunlight glinted, briefly, on the water of the lake; a couple of energetic joggers puffed their way round the perimeter path. Then the sight was lost to view.

He put his foot down harder, and wound up the window. "Breakfast in Newmarket?"

Marjorie screwed up her face. "God, no. Not Newmarket."

"Okay, then, early lunch at the pub in Thetford."

"That sounds more like it."

"Then on to Mac's lot by two-thirty. No sweat."

The University of East Anglia was not a prepossessing sight. The weather-beaten blocks of the student residences looked more like a prison camp than a seat of learning, and the long, gray building housing the university's academic departments, streaked with dark splotches from a recent heavy thunderstorm, reminded him of an old ship tied up in harbor. He couldn't imagine why an architect would have designed such a monstrosity, or who let him get away with it. The great slab of gray stretched away from the reasonably pleasant little square where eating places, bookshop, students' union, and administrative buildings were grouped, and seemed designed to catch the wind which always seemed to be blowing across the park. Its only redeeming feature, as far as Richard could see, was that it provided a means of walking under cover almost all the way down to the Sainsbury Center, the great hangarlike building that housed a surprisingly good collection of seventies and eighties art.

They'd just caught the last of the rain, running across from the car park, then it had cleared and they mounted the steps to the elevated walkway which ran down the side of the main building.

"How do you know which bit you want?" Marjorie had never been to this campus before.

"Easy. First door past the computer center." He pointed. "That's the square block on the left. But don't ask me where anything else is!"

Inside the first door past the computer block there was a lobby area, stretching across the entire width of the building. A few chairs and tables were scattered about, and a tall man with dark hair, just flecked with gray, was studying, or pretending to study, a large wall chart showing details of sea levels worldwide at the time of the breakup of the West Antarctic ice sheet, 125,000 years ago.

He turned as the breeze from the opened door blew across the lobby. His bright blue eyes, startling with the dark hair, darted about, birdlike, taking in the scene. He smiled. "Dick— dead on time—as always."

Richard held out his hand. "Hi, Mac. This is Marjorie—Marjorie Cooper. Marjorie, this is Bill MacRobyn. What's with the lurking in the corridors, Mac? Worried about rising sea level?" He gestured at the chart.

"You'd better believe it. Nearly two centimeters in the past decade."

As he spoke, MacRobyn nodded to Marjorie and shook her hand. Then he took Richard by the elbow and steered him down one of the long corridors.

"But I know that stuff by heart. I wanted to catch you before anyone else did. I had a word with Stephens, and he's all for it. In fact, he's been having lunch with Rogers, trying to butter him up."

"Rogers?"

"Admin. He has to rubber-stamp everything. If he says okay, we don't have to put it through a full council meeting, and we can avoid any hassles. I hope. You see, Dick, Cambridge isn't the only place where people get leaned on from above. That stuff on the news last night, it wasn't good. The girl who claimed you tried to run her over, all the rest of it. Well, I'm not sure that the council would extend an offer to you to take up an official post here."

"But all I need is lab space, for a couple—"

MacRobyn cut his protest short. "Don't worry. If you don't need any money . . ."

Dick shook his head.

"And you're officially on sabbatical from Cambridge, not doing any new work, then we can fix it. Nobody outside Stephens's team, except me and Rogers, need know you're here, or who you are, or what you're doing. We've got to get something in writing, just because you've become a hot potato. But all we need is a letter from Rogers giving you emeritus status as a temporary member of Stephens's group. It's no problem, really it isn't. But I didn't want you leaping about all over the place, spreading the glad tidings of your imminent move to Norwich. Keep it low-key, and tactful. By the time anyone complains, you'll have finished your work, anyway."

Be calm, Richard thought to himself. Be reasonable, be pleasant, be polite.

"Don't worry, Mac. I've learned a few things in the past few days. You won't even notice that I'm here."

MacRobyn was clearly relieved at the lack of any prima-donna temperament. "Great. Look, I had to get the message across. It's not as if you've got a big reputation for anything else, in the outside world, I mean. People only know you as the crazy blasphemer—I'm sorry, but it's true. And we have to work around that. Once the smoke clears, though—if you're looking for a new base—well, Stephens might have something to put to you, later on.

"Here we are." He stopped at a door. "Would you like me to entertain Dr. Cooper—"

"Marjorie, please."

"Okay, Marjorie. Do you want to see the sights while Dick beards the lion in his den?"

She looked at Dick, who looked in turn at MacRobyn.

"I think it's best. Low-key, person to person. A small, insignificant little proposal, just granting you library rights and a key to Stephens's lab, nothing special. You know the form, Dick, just make like a fresh PhD seeking his first job."

Dick nodded. "Fine. Marjorie will be better off with you. It won't be a pretty sight, seeing the new me at work, licking boots and arses in all directions. I'll see you in the coffee shop, then?"

Be calm, be reasonable.

MacRobyn nodded and turned to go. Marjorie placed her hand, lightly, on Richard's arm. "Take care, Dick. I'll find out if there's a good restaurant where we can celebrate your new status, later."

He smiled and nodded, then leaned forward and kissed her, lightly on the lips, before turning back to the door.

Sixteen

They found the restaurant, and the meal was good. They did have something to celebrate—in Richard's wallet, carefully tucked away, a formal letter from Rogers, offering Richard the status of an unpaid, honorary visiting research Fellow, for the next two terms, as a member of the genetic biology research group. It was dated two days earlier; Richard's reply, carrying yesterday's date, in which he accepted the offer, was already in Rogers's files. Richard had typed it himself, on the micro in Stephens's lab. Everything aboveboard, official but low-key, a routine matter dealt with routinely, *before*, according to the files, Dr. Richard Lee showed signs of becoming persona non grata.

The need for the little subterfuge grated, but he'd kept up his affable exterior, agreeing to everything, congratulating everyone on their wisdom, aching to get away and be alone with Marjorie again. He'd drunk most of the bottle of wine they'd shared with the meal, of course, so she was driving back. Probably a breach of the rental agreement, thought Richard with satisfaction, if he'd actually had a rental agreement. But who was to say what was and was not part of the deal when he'd merely borrowed a courtesy car?

It wasn't really late—eleven o'clock and they were already nearly home. But he was glad of the efficient heater in the old car, which combined with the meal and the wine to produce a warm glow both inside and outside his body. I'm pretty good at arse-licking, Richard told himself, reflecting back on the day's proceedings. Maybe I should try for a career in administration myself. Or politics.

He chuckled quietly to himself.

"Share the joke?" Marjorie asked.

"Just thinking I ought to be a politician. Champion crawler and bootlicker extraordinaire."

"No way. You're too honest."

"Thanks for the compliment."

"Where do I turn?" Marjorie had slowed the car, checking for the right turning onto the old road through the villages.

"Don't bother. Go right up to the roundabout and in from the top end, as if you were coming from Cambridge."

"Okay." She picked up speed again, changing down to accelerate and then up again as the little car gathered momentum. At the brightly lit roundabout, they turned in a full three-quarters of a circle, pointing back the way they had come, before turning off, to the left, into the dark lane that led into the village. Once again she changed deftly through the gears, beginning a last sprint down the mile or so of the home stretch. The sudden stab of bright, full-beam headlights facing them, on their own side of the road, shocked Richard into full awareness. He observed, clearly and with time to spare, as events unfolded in slow motion. Marjorie started to brake, then swerved onto the other side of the lane, then braked again as the dark bulk of an unlit vehicle loomed in front of them. There was no way to avoid it. They hit with a smash of glass, and Richard felt the strap of his seat belt bite deep into his shoulder as he was flung forward. He tasted salty blood. Bitten my lip, he thought, groggily. Get out. Fire risk. Marjorie had already turned off the ignition, pulled the key from its lock, and was unfastening her seat belt. She turned, it seemed very slowly, to look at him.

"Are you . . ."

Suddenly, the world snapped back into place, moving at its proper speed. The driver's door was wrenched open, and a gloved hand reached in, hauling Marjorie out of the vehicle. Richard pushed at his own, jammed door, then smashed against it with all the weight of his shoulder. He half fell out of the car, cracking his head on the pillar of the door as it suddenly gave way, and sprawling into the road.

"What the fuck?"

A voice from the other side of the vehicle. Running feet.

"It ain't him. Some old bird."

Richard shook his head. Things were moving slowly again.

Another voice. "Round here! I've got the bastard!"

Richard was half standing, supporting himself on the door of the car, when the first boot took him in the back of the knee, making him collapse once again onto the road. Another took him in the back of the head, and he huddled, instinctively, into a ball, arms over his face, while they thudded into his back. One smashed into the fingers of his left hand, curled over his right ear. But he felt no pain, and a small, logical part of his brain, curled up inside his head, calmly took note of the fact, for future reference.

"Leave him alone!"

Marjorie's voice! The small, logical part of his brain swung into action.

"Run, Marjorie! Get the hell out of here!"

"Shut up, fuckface."

Another boot thudded into his back.

"What about the bird?" The kicking stopped. Richard uncurled slightly, moving his hands so that he could see what was going on, by the still blazing lights of the car parked, as he now realized, on the other side of the road. A setup, he thought. I've been set up. Again. A stab of pain shot up his left arm, and, as if it were a cue, a chorus of aches began to penetrate from his back to his brain. He felt sick.

Two men, wearing dark knit caps that obscured their features, were holding Marjorie, laughing as she tried to kick out at them. A third, who had obviously just delivered the final kick to Richard, had turned and was walking slowly toward them.

"She's a game old girl."

Her blouse had been torn partly open by the struggle, buttons bursting off their thread and revealing a flash of her breasts as she moved in the bright lights.

"Got nice tits. I know what I'd like to do to her." They laughed again.

Richard was on his hands and knees. Correction; *hand* and knees. The left one didn't seem to be much good. Got to do something, he thought, as the third tough moved right up to the still struggling Marjorie. Suddenly, she spat, full in his face.

"You cunt!" His half-jocular manner changed in a flash, the thug punched her, hard, full in the stomach. She slumped forward, falling to the ground, retching, as the other two let go of her arms.

"Cunt." A statement, almost matter of fact, as he kicked her, hard, on the side of her head. It was a full swing of the boot, making a sickening crunch on impact. She stopped moving. The other two joined in, kicking in desultory fashion at the now still body for a few seconds, then turning their attention back to where Richard was struggling to rise to his feet.

"C'mon, that's it. Mess him up, they said. Make sure he gets the message."

The largest of the three men walked back to Richard, now leaning on the roof of the car, while his companions got into their own vehicle.

"The message is this, mister smartarse. We don't want you round here. Or your fancy woman. And we don't want no more of this muck about monkeys and nignogs being our brothers. Next time, it's knives. Right?"

He signed off the message with a right into the pit of Richard's stomach. Richard collapsed onto the ground once again, receiving a last kick to his now undefended head, and lapsing into unconsciousness as he heard, vaguely, the sound of a car departing at high speed.

Occasional flashes of the outside world penetrated. Lights and sirens; being lifted. The face of a nurse.

"Marjorie?"

"Just relax. Your friend is being attended to."

A rattling trolley. More lights, in a corridor. Another nurse—or was it the same one? The stab of a needle in his left arm. Then, nothing.

Seventeen

The first thing he saw when he woke was his own left forearm and hand, swathed in white, suspended on a cradle in front of him. He was lying on his back, in a hospital bed. His head hurt. Exploring with his right hand, he felt the bandages. At least his eyes were all right. His back hurt. He wondered if anything else was broken, and tried wiggling his toes.

"Feeling better, Dr. Lee?"

A nurse, with a clipboard and a glass of pink liquid.

"Drink this." She placed the glass in his good hand, and made a note.

"How's Marjorie?"

"Drink up, please, Dr. Lee."

He obliged, while she watched.

"Dr. Cooper isn't on this ward. She's being looked after by someone else, but I'll find out how she is for you." The rules were clear. If he was a good boy and drank his medicine, she would take notice of his requests. If not, tough.

"There's a policeman waiting to see you, Dr. Lee. Do you feel up to it?"

He started to nod, then thought better of it. "What's the time?"

"Ten in the morning. And it's Tuesday. You've been out of things for a few days." She smiled, brightly, as if this was a piece of good news, and departed. A man in a blue suit, anonymous, nondescript, replaced her and sat down on the bedside chair.

"Dr. Lee? I'm Sergeant Warren. I'd like to get some details of the accident from you, sir, while it's still fresh in your mind." He pulled a notebook from his pocket, and waited, expectantly.

"It was no bloody accident, Sergeant, that's for sure!"

"Sir?"

Weakly at first, but with gathering strength as the recollection sent a surge of adrenaline through his body, Richard recounted how the setup had been arranged.

"So you think, sir, that your assailants intended you to crash into the stationary vehicle?"

"Yes."

"And you believe that they were expressly looking for you, to deliver this warning?"

He nodded, in spite of the headache.

"Miss Cooper—I'm sorry, *Doctor* Cooper, she was driving?"

"Yes, I told you."

"And who owns the vehicle, sir?"

"Marshall's." The thought of the thousand-pound check came back to him. "At least, they did."

"Sir?"

"We had an arrangement. An insurance problem. Don't worry. I'm covered for third party. But I left a check with them, so that if anything happened to the car they could cash it and I'd get to keep the car. I guess it's mine now. What's left of it."

"I see." He made a note.

"Can you explain how the assailants knew you were in that car?"

An image flashed into his mind. The rearview mirror; a police car with a uniformed driver talking into a microphone; to one side, a scruffy demonstrator, writing in a notebook.

"Yes, I can. We used the car in the morning, going to the Institute. One of the demonstrators there made a note of the number; I saw him." Richard was beginning to feel much more alert, in spite of the aches and pains. Maybe that pink stuff was a pick-me-up.

"It would've been easy for them to pick us up in the lights at the roundabout, signal down the lane. Bugger it. If only we'd come in by the back road, the way Marjorie wanted to.

"Look, do you know how Marjorie is? Have you spoken to her? She'll back me up." He realized how ridiculous his story must sound.

"I'm afraid I haven't been able to speak to her, sir." Sergeant Warren looked up from his notebook. "She's not conscious. But you don't have to worry about anything from my point of view. The car you hit was stolen earlier that same day, in Histon. Not far from the Institute where you work. And the injuries inflicted on both you and your companion are certainly consistent with the story you've told. We aren't going to charge you with anything, but I have to warn you it's not very likely we'll find out who did it."

Relief and concern mixed in Richard's mind. At least neither he nor Marjorie was going to get charged with reckless driving. But she was still unconscious—well, he'd only just come round himself, and he felt all right now, more or less. She'd be up and about any minute. After all, she'd taken a nasty kick just at the end.

All of the relief washed away, leaving only anxiety. He closed his eyes, and both saw and heard that vicious kick to Marjorie's head.

The policeman was still looking at him when he opened his eyes. "Is Marjorie badly hurt?"

"I'm not the expert, Dr. Lee. But here's someone that is."

He stood up and shook hands with the new arrival, a white-coated woman.

"I think the patient has probably had enough of you for the time being, Sergeant."

"He's asking after Dr. Cooper, the other victim of the incident."

Incident! Richard raged inwardly, then calmed. Just police training. Everything is an "incident" to them.

The doctor looked at Richard, then reached over to take his pulse. Playing for time, he thought. The sergeant left.

"How's Marjorie?"

"I really don't have any good news for you, Dr. Lee."

"It's Richard. Or Dick." He replied automatically. "How bad is it, then?"

"Very bad."

There was a silence.

"If I thought it would help your own recovery, Richard, I'd lie to you. But I don't think there's any need. You've got two broken fingers, which are healing nicely now they're set, you've been concussed, got cracked ribs, and no doubt you can tell me more about the bruises than I can tell you. You'll make a splendid recovery in a very short time. Let's be in no doubt about that.

"But the news I have about your friend is the worst I could bring you." She paused.

"Marjorie Cooper died two days ago."

He'd guessed what was coming, from her buildup. The trained, professional bedside manner, the small, logical part of his brain reminded him. Break the news gently, so the recipient already knows what's coming before you spell it out.

"How?"

"It was a combination of things." The doctor nodded to the nurse, who started preparing another glass of pinkish liquid. "She lost a lot of blood, even before the ambulance reached you. The result of blows to the abdomen. Is it possible she was in the early stages of pregnancy?"

"Yes. A few weeks."

"I'm sorry. And she had a depressed fracture of the skull. I overheard you talking to the sergeant just now, but we'd already worked out what caused that." She waited, while the nurse offered the drink to Richard. He took it obediently.

"If we could have operated immediately, we might have been able to sort that out. But we had to give her massive transfusions first, and try to stop the bleeding. In the end, we *had* to operate on the head injury. She died while I was doing so. I'm sorry."

"Thank you." It took guts, and a bit more than professional bedside manner, for the surgeon to come here in person to tell him how Marjorie had died. On that same surgeon's operating table. Goddammit, he'd respect that courage and be polite. And he *wouldn't* burst out in tears like some hysterical child. The dampness down his cheek must be where he'd spilled some of that bloody drink.

The nurse made another note on her clipboard. "Better rest now, Dr. Lee." She turned and followed the doctor to the desk at the end of the room, where they stood for a moment, discussing something. Probably me, thought Richard, as a woolly vagueness began to creep over him. He still felt the pain, but as if it belonged to someone else. The small, logical part of his brain was in control again. It was, of course, all his fault, he told himself, logically. If he hadn't agreed to do the implant, she wouldn't have been losing blood at such a rate. If he hadn't agreed to take her to Norwich for the day, she wouldn't even have *been* there. And if he hadn't got his damn fool face on TV showing off about his work nobody would have known, or cared, and he could have stayed in a quiet academic rut forever.

It was quite clear. Marjorie's death was a punishment, to him, for showing off. And also a reminder to him, not to make cozy plans involving other people. He was his own man, all right, and when he got out of here he'd stay that way.

* * *

He didn't really sleep, but stayed in a half-awake, daydreaming state, watching the comings and goings of the ward, making foolish plans for the future. A future in which he would pull up the drawbridge of his castle and live alone, ignoring the world and getting on with his own experiments, publishing nothing but leaving it all for posterity. Let *them* suffer the backlash from the mob. He'd had enough.

It was all foolishness, of course, the logical part of his brain reminded him. Where would he get the money to build his castle with?

It might have been a couple of hours later that the nurse returned.

"Are you awake, Dr. Lee?"

He grunted at her. Stupid woman. She didn't think he slept with his eyes open, did she?

"There's a telephone call for you, from a Dr. Cobb. He says it's good news. Would you like to take the call?"

Good news? From John Cobb? The last person he wanted to speak to was John Cobb. But the nurse was still there, smiling brightly. Poor thing. She only wanted to cheer him up. No point in making trouble. Be polite, be calm, be reasonable.

He tried to smile back. "Why not?"

She nodded, and trotted off to her desk, returning with the handset, antenna already extended. He struggled to sit more upright, and she placed the phone on the bed while she helped him, plumping up pillows behind his back and rearranging the arm cradle. Then she placed the phone in his right hand.

He thumbed the button. "John? This is Dick.

I hope it really is good news, I need some right now."

"Dick!" Cobb really did sound excited. "You picked just the right time to start sitting up and taking notice!" His voice changed, to a mixture of embarrassment and formality. "We were all very sorry to hear about Marjorie Cooper, Dick. Everyone knows you two went back a long way together." So it was public knowledge, already. "Uh, commiserations." He was only trying to be polite, he'd hardly known Marjorie.

"Thank you, John. What's the news? Or did you just call to offer condolences?"

"It's real news, Dick. The Big One." Excitement was beginning to creep back into Cobb's voice. "It'll be official in about two hours from now. It's the Nobel, Dick! For physiology or medicine!"

"What do you mean?"

"The prize, idiot. For you and me. Today!"

The Nobel Prize? This was utterly crazy. Maybe he'd died in that car crash, and didn't know it yet. Maybe he was still unconscious. What on earth had that nurse put in the pink drink last time? People simply didn't get Nobels for years and years after they'd done their work.

"Dick—are you still there?"

"Yeah, I'm here."

"You don't sound too pleased. Look, Dick, I have to say this, I know it's all because of the bad time you've been having. The citation as good as says so—they say it's for our 'major contribution to the alleviation of human suffering around the world.' And there's some stuff about the need for nations to stand together not only to combat plague and pestilence, but also to combat the rising tide of unreason and antiscience. Strong stuff. It's a swipe at the government, Dick, using us as political pawns.

"Hell, I don't care as long as we get the prize. Two hundred kay between us, and all the prestige you can eat. But it wouldn't be a worthwhile gesture if it weren't for you being a public figure. So it's an ill wind, eh?"

Cobb's delight was getting the better of him now that he'd got the news off his chest.

"But how, John?" Richard felt as deflated as Cobb sounded high. "The nominations had to be in months ago, before all this blew up . . ."

"Yeah, would you believe it, someone had enough sense to nominate us as soon as the *J. Mol. Biol.* paper came out. Beckenstein, over in San Francisco. Of course. he was just riding his own hobby horse. Never thought we'd get it. But then, comes time for the committee meeting, someone decides it would be fun to poke Britain and the rest of Europe with a sharp stick, to kick back at all this neo-Christian stuff, and our names came to the top of the heap."

"Oh, sure. Politics." That made sense, the logical part of his brain told him. You'd never expect to win a Nobel Prize on merit, would you? But as part of someone else's political game, why, of course it made sense. The literature prize had been a political football for decades. About time science got in on the act.

"You can write your own ticket now, Dick. They'll have you back at the Institute with open arms. Or anywhere else for that matter. Dick?"

He wasn't listening. The hand holding the

phone lay on the bed, and he thumbed the button to cut off the tiny voice. Tears started to roll quietly down both cheeks, as the pink liquid wore off sufficiently for him to remember the *really* important thing that had happened in the past week. He hadn't been with Marjorie, holding her hand, at the moment she died.

Interlude:
EXODUS II

Eighteen

Year Six

Birds fascinated Adam. They came and went as they pleased, through the air. Doors didn't interest him so much. Doors simply led into rooms, and he knew all about rooms. He didn't mind that Uncle Dick and Nanny went into rooms he didn't go in, through doors he couldn't open. Who needed more rooms and doors, anyway?

He was glad that Uncle Dick and Nanny had each other to play with, when he wasn't with them. He didn't want them to be lonely, in the rooms they shared beyond the door he couldn't open. He was sure they were happy, now. It was hard to remember how things used to be, when he was small. But he didn't remember Uncle Dick smiling very much, then. Now, he smiled a lot, and laughed. When they all went for a walk together, Adam still often walked in the

middle, holding Nanny's hand on one side and
Uncle Dick's on the other, while they went to
see the flowers in the garden. Sometimes,
though, Uncle Dick walked in the middle, holding hands with Nanny and with Adam.

Adam didn't mind. He wanted Uncle Dick and
Nanny to be happy together. One day, he was
going to follow the birds, over the wall, far
away. He couldn't go if the grown-ups would be
sad without him. But if they were happy in their
rooms, it wouldn't matter if he went exploring
for a while.

Nineteen

"*This* is the way it was written in the Bible!" The white-haired evangelist raised the Holy Book on high, in his left hand, to be sure that none of his audience could mistake it. But he quoted the words without reading them, as if they were engraved in letters of fire in his soul.

"The Lord saw that the wickedness of man was great in the earth, and that every imagination of the thoughts of his heart was only evil.

"My friends, can you doubt the word of the Lord, and His wisdom?"

A roar came back from the congregation: "No!"

"Now the earth was corrupt in God's sight, and the earth was filled with violence.

"My friends, can you doubt that such evil times have come again?"

"No!"

"So what did our Lord do, to cleanse the world of its evil and wicked ways? He sent a flood. He sent rain upon the earth forty days and forty nights, and every living thing that He had made, He did blot out from the face of the ground. The fountains of the great deep burst forth, and the windows of heaven were opened, and the rain fell upon the earth forty days and forty nights, and the world was cleansed.

"My friends." The voice dropped to the conspiratorial whisper that, thanks to modern electronic technology, was conveyed with perfect clarity to every listener. "My friends, the scientists tell us that the sea is rising. Every day we hear news of flood and tempest striking in the low-lying regions of the globe. The scientists tell us that this is no supernatural phenomenon, but simply the natural consequence of human actions, warming the world as we burn its resources and destroy its forests.

"But I say unto you"—the voice rising now, slowly but steadily, to a new climax—"I say unto you, my friends, that this is no more and no less than our God-given just desserts, the reward for tampering with knowledge that is forbidden us by God. The Lord himself cleansed the earth once with a great flood; can any rightthinking man or woman doubt that He is warning us now to mend our ways, before we are overwhelmed by the new flood?

"But it is not too late. The Lord *is* merciful. There is still time, if we have the will, to turn our backs on the evils of technology and be saved. Do *you* want to be saved?"

"Yes!"

"Praise the Lord!"

"Hallelujah!"

The cries mingled in a wild mixture of noise as the audience rose to its feet, applauding and cheering. The message was getting through.

In the north of Zimbabwe, a small group of well-disciplined soldiers, in recognizable, clean but ragged uniforms, was systematically burning an entire village. A few of the soldiers wore gas masks; the rest had wet rags tied around their mouths and noses. Huts, some containing bodies, were doused with gasoline from jerry cans; brushwood was piled at the doors. When everyone was clear, an officer walked through the small group of huts with a blazing brand, thrusting it at each doorway in turn. The men watched, in exhausted silence, from the shade of the two trucks. When everything was burning fiercely, the officer returned, and gestured for the squad to mount up. As they climbed into the backs of the lorries, he reached into the open door of the lead vehicle, from which a long whip aerial pointed to the sky, and pulled out a hand microphone on a coiled lead.

"Delta leader, this is Cleanup Two."

"We read you, Cleanup Two. Awaiting your report."

"We've finished here. Heading out now for the rendezvous at the Hunyani River crossing."

"Understood, Two. Make it snappy. As of now, we've got permission to cross into Mozambique, but the word is the border's being sealed soon. Captain Mandela says they'll need us anyway, with our experience out here, but I wouldn't want to bet on it."

"Roger, Leader. Don't worry. We don't want

to stay here one moment longer than we have to. Signing out."

He replaced the microphone, and waved his arm in a circular motion above his head. The drivers of the two lorries started their engines, and as the officer climbed into his seat they were already bumping off across the dusty hillside, heading east.

The latest of the plagues breaking out from the north and west had defeated them, pushing back the line of human settlement another few score miles. In the late 1980s it had been AIDS, bursting out of war-torn Uganda and killing one in ten of the adult population before it halted, for no known reason, no more than 250 miles southwest of Lake Tanganyika. Then Kawambwa syndrome, named after the town where it was first identified, with its violent retching, diarrhea, and almost inevitable death by dehydration. Now, the plague known simply as "the cough," starting as no more than a dry hacking, developing within a week into full-blown coughing of blood-specked phlegm, ending, in more than half of all known cases, in death by asphyxiation as the lungs filled with fluid.

The human heart was being torn out of Africa, with civilization retreating back to the coastal fringes. Zaire, Zambia, Uganda, and most of Tanzania were now more mysterious to man than in the days of Stanley and Livingstone, while the Cape remained a radioactive no-go area, destroyed by the final revenge of the black community on their white oppressors. The last recognizable, organized national government in Africa south of Sudan was in the process of trying, vainly, to draw a protective belt around itself, as it huddled in the coastal plains of Mozambique.

For many species, not prone to the same diseases that ravaged mankind, this was very much a change for the better. Herds of many kinds of deer spread out from the untended national parks, and roamed once more across the plains, tracked and preyed upon by a small, but increasing, number of great cats. Giraffe found fresh greenery to browse upon in the plantations abandoned by man, while hippos wallowed unmolested in the rivers and lakes. With increased rainfall, the semiarid regions on the edge of the great forests became wetter, encouraging the jungle to begin the slow and painful process of reaching out to reclaim the territory that had once been its own. And from the trees, foraging out boldly in small bands during the daytime, gathering together in the branches for safety by night, alert and intelligent, with no enemies that couldn't be chased off by weight of numbers or outclimbed among the trees, the chimpanzees began to undergo a major population explosion. They ate freely of the fruits of the trees, and as the trees spread, so too did they.

Twenty

Year Seven

Adam's sixth birthday was a big success. Nanny made him a cake with six candles on, and his name spelled out in red icing. Of course, Nanny was always nice. He couldn't remember a time before she'd been around to look after him when Uncle Dick was busy, helping with his bath, cooking, and just being there.

He liked the computer Uncle Dick had given him for his birthday, because it had lots of games to play on it. Uncle Dick said he'd show Adam how to make up new games for himself, and teach the computer how to play them, but he didn't know how to do that yet. In fact, the best new toy was the construction kit, with lots of yellow plastic rods and girders that fastened together with red nuts and bolts to make almost anything you wanted. Adam spent most of his birthday afternoon deeply engrossed with the kit, carefully studying the clear diagrams and pictures that came with it; he couldn't read very well yet, but he understood how to fit the different shapes together to make them match the pictures.

Once the little electric motor was secured in place, and the batteries slotted into the hole on top of the motor, the truck ought to work.

His tongue licked out of the corner of his mouth as he concentrated on his task. Over by the window, Nanny and Uncle Dick were drinking tea. Adam put the model truck down, and picked up the plan, frowning slightly as he painstakingly compared his effort with the illustrations. Satisfied, he nodded to himself, then glanced over at the adults. They didn't seem to be paying him much attention. Smiling, he lined the truck up on Nanny's right foot, under the table, and moved the lever on the motor. With a faint whine from the little motor, the wheels began to turn and the truck edged forward.

"Finished!" Adam shouted. "Look out, Nanny! It's coming to get you!"

Feigning surprise, squealing, Nanny pulled her foot out of the way as the truck brushed up against it. But Uncle Dick, peering around the side of the table, carefully placed his own foot in the truck's path. The right-hand wheels of the vehicle lifted over his toes, the truck tilting dangerously to the left but mounting the obstacle and settling back on a level path, continuing until it hit the wall under the window.

Laughing, Uncle Dick reached down and turned the truck around, heading it back toward Adam.

"Very good, Adam! We'll have to get you a job as an engineer."

Twenty miles north of Ahmadabad, a large, dusty red truck was bouncing its way toward the outskirts of Kalol. Headlights blazing, horn blasting, it forced a way through the stream of traffic and refugees flooding the other way, bouncing off the road proper onto the dry fields on either side wherever necessary to make progress. The driver spent most of his time leaning from the cab window, gesticulating with his free hand and shouting in Hindi. On the other side of the vehicle, his companion did the same.

At last, the flow of refugee traffic, on foot, pushing handcarts, in a variety of battered vehicles, began to ease. He pulled his head back into the vehicle, and shouted instead at the driver, above the roar of the engine, "How much farther?"

The driver shrugged, changing up a gear as a stretch of clear road opened up ahead. "Five miles; no more. You will see the reactor building when we cross over the next rise."

At the top of that rise, there was an army roadblock. Two trucks, parked at an angle to one another across the road so that another vehicle could maneuver past them only slowly and with care. They stopped, and the passenger showed his credentials.

"Is the area clear inside?"

The young lieutenant spread his hands in a gesture of ignorance.

"I'm sorry, sir. I have no information. Our instructions are to let anyone pass who wants to

get out of the immediate vicinity, but to let nobody in without written authorization. The fire
is still burning. We are expecting to be relieved
by a platoon with radiation equipment at any
time now."

He hoped they would be—and that the protective gear he had requested was waiting for
him down the road.

"Okay." He pulled his head back into the
truck and nodded to the driver, who inched past
the obstacles and headed down the road again.
Smoke from the big, square building ahead of
them rose almost vertically into the clear sky.
Just about halfway between the checkpoint and
the burning building, a cluster of vehicles were
grouped together, with people, some in the dis-
tinctive white of protective clothing, dotted
among them.

"Looks like that's where we stop. Get the
equipment unloaded, while I suit up and find
out what's going on."

It was the driver's turn to nod and mutter
"Okay."

Several people had gathered to await the
truck's approach. The passenger swung the
door open and jumped down before it had
stopped moving, to be greeted by a short, plump
man who welcomed him warmly, flinging his
arms, incongruously, around the taller man.

"Chandra! I'm delighted to see you. And
you've brought the equipment. Very good."

"Sunil, you old fox. They told me you were
trapped inside. Done for."

The little man took off his glasses and rubbed
them, carefully, on the sleeve of his shirt. Re-

placing them, he squinted up at his companion, a serious expression on his face.

"I'm afraid half the rumor is true, Chandra. I'm certainly done for. All of us in the control room at the time. Well, it's just a matter of time."

He held up a hand to ward off Chandra's expressions of sympathy.

"No, no. No time for any of that. Let's take it as said, shall we, and get on with the job at hand. I can brief you while you suit up."

They walked over to a white trailer truck, Sunil talking swiftly as they did so.

"We know exactly what happened, even though we don't know why. In the Number Two core, there was a blowout in the steam tubes. The safety failed, and we had a jet of steam spraying the graphite. At those temperatures, well"—a little shrug of the round shoulders— "it's the old water-gas reaction, the one they said could never happen here. Hydrogen and carbon monoxide given off, then something ignited the gases. The explosion cracked the lid, but there's very little contamination. The outer building did its job. But the fire—well, that's your department."

Chandra was already stripping off his outer garments and climbing, feet first, into the one-piece radiation suit.

"So the smoke's not as serious as it looks?"

"Not in terms of radiation. The roof is only cracked, and there was little upward blast. Local fallout, of course, but nothing much outside the immediate vicinity."

"What happened to the water dumps?"

Again, the gesture of incomprehension, ignorance.

"They failed. We don't know why. In training, we were always told at least six things would have to go wrong together to produce any kind of hazard. Well, all I can say is six things *have* gone wrong together."

"Sabotage?"

"Who knows?"

Chandra had finished suiting up, but had the face plate of his helmet open.

"I'll go in alone, first, to assess the situation. I'll need a driver—"

"Myself. I have nothing to lose—no, no Chandra, it's definite. I'm good for a few more hours yet, so I'll do what I can for as long as I can. And fill you in a bit more on the drive."

Chandra smiled.

"Okay, Sunil. The old team, eh? One last time?"

Sunil smiled back.

"One last time, old friend."

While the two Indians were bouncing toward the burning reactor building in their jeep, 180 tons of uranium oxide, initially at a temperature of 700 degrees centigrade, was beginning to melt down inside the building, as the fire in the graphite control rods destroyed the careful geometry of the pile and allowed neutrons from the decay of uranium atoms to slam almost unhindered into their neighbors, triggering further atomic decays and releasing more heat in the process. There was no chance of the core becoming involved in a runaway fission reaction and turning into a bomb, but without the moderating influence of the graphite the heat being generated by the fission process was already far in excess of that produced by the flames. At 2,700 degrees centigrade, uranium oxide itself was beginning to melt and puddle together, hotter than the melting point of anything around it, hotter than the melting point of steel, or concrete.

At those temperatures, the concrete of the floor of the building was already being broken down into its constituent parts, into carbon, sulphur, and oxygen. Consumed by fierce chemical reactions, these materials added to the smoke pouring from the cracked roof of the building, and the mass of molten, radioactive material on the floor began to eat its way downward into the ground.

It was while the little jeep was bouncing back along the road, away from the reactor, after Chandra had completed his brief survey of the situation, that the molten mass encountered water.

The plain of the Gujarat region around Ahmadabad is relatively well supplied with water, by Indian standards. Not very much lying around on the surface, true, but rivers drain off from the Aravalli Range to the northeast, and from the Vindhya Range to the east, into the Gulf of Kuch and the Gulf of Cambay. The water table is not too far below the surface—not too far, that is for the furiously hot, molten mass of self-heating uranium oxide to reach in a matter of hours after the accident.

When water encounters a mass of molten material at a temperature of several thousand degrees, it cannot quench the heat. Instead, a tiny fraction of the heat stored in the molten mass flashes the water into steam in a fraction of a second. Expanding fiercely underground, the steam blasts its way to the surface explosively, forming craters and scattering the molten droplets far and wide. The effect is like an earthquake, or a short-lived, but violent, volcanic eruption.

The observers grouped around the cluster of vehicles watched in horror as the jeep went bouncing out of control, turning end over end and scattering its two occupants as the shock wave hit it. Almost simultaneously, a crack appeared in the wall of the building of Number Two reactor, and parts of the structure collapsed inward. As the rumble of the explosions reached the watchers, a new and deadlier cloud of smoke belched from the ruined building and rose into the sky. Part of the structure of the Number One building collapsed in the background, almost without fuss; and the flames, fanned by the easier flow of air through the ruined structures, began to spread out toward the Number One reactor core.

On the little ridge, five miles away from the reactor complex, the soldiers on roadblock duty turned from their brew of char, looking up as the explosion rumbled past them. After a moment of stunned silence, most of them started to run for the trucks. As the engine of the first truck started, the lieutenant opened the driver's door, pulling out his pistol with his free hand.

"Wait! I order you to stop! There are people back there who need help!"

A soldier jumped down from the back of the

second truck, and raised his rifle. A single shot
sent the lieutenant sprawling in the road, his
pistol flying out of his hand. The first truck was
already moving off, south; as the murderer
jumped back into the second truck it too began
to move, straight ahead down the road, bumping over the dead man's legs as it went on its
way.

Twenty-one

Year Eight

"Prime Minister . . ." The figure standing at the tall window, staring out into the garden, didn't move.

"Sir . . ." The aide shut the door, carefully using a little more force than was really necessary. The sharp sound penetrated where politeness had failed, and the Prime Minister turned, startled out of his reverie.

"Frank! What time is it?"

"Half an hour before we have to leave for the studios, sir. I've got the final text with me. We can run through it now, in case you want to make any last-minute alterations."

The older man waved the suggestion away, with a tired gesture.

"No, Frank, it's too late for any of that now. We've made our commitment, God help us, and all we can do is explain it to the masses. The worst thing is, they'll probably be delighted.''

There really had been no choice, he reminded himself, even though it did stick in the throat to carry the measures through. He knew there'd be no dissent in Parliament—the Leader of the Opposition had already agreed, privately, that the interests of the nation were synonymous, now, with the interests of Europe. "Fortress Europe," that's what they were already calling it, on the box and in the papers. Inevitable, really, with the American withdrawal and the increasing isolationism of the new administration in Washington. The new European Armed Forces, with a unified structure and a single chain of command, was the only logical response to the new threat from the East. But the cost! Paying for it was going to be painful, and although one of the lesser immediate pains was the cutting of all foreign aid—well, he feared that was a symptom of a deeper ill than he had any hope of curing in his time in office. His standing in the opinion polls would, undoubtedly, rise after tonight's broadcast, and the bill would probably go through unopposed in the House. At last, the media would say, the government was putting Britain, and Europe, first. The whole nation was united behind him—and it was the unhappiest moment of his political career.

The thump of large-caliber guns to the rear was followed by the loud crack of starshell and parachute flares igniting, drifting down from the sky. The harsh light illuminated the scene of past battles, with the remains of tanks and other vehicles littering the desert, and a few shell holes still visible, outlines softened by the drifting sand.

In a long, ragged line across the battlefront, a mass of figures stood and began to run across the sand, screaming as they went, a long, drawn-out cry,

"Allaaaaaaaah!"

Automatic weapons opened up on them as they ran. Even blinded by the light between them and the running figures, the operators of the weapons couldn't fail to find targets among the mass of humanity surging toward them. Figures fell to the sand, some lying still where they fell, others struggling, crying out, attempting to crawl forward, firing their own weapons for a time in spite of their wounds. But the more that fell, the more seemed to appear, as if out of the ground, to replace them. The trenches and weapons positions were overrun by sheer weight of numbers.

Dawn showed the battlefield still littered with corpses, a few precious, scarce tanks being maneuvered forward and concealed in the new lines, almost a mile advanced from their previous positions. The tanks, with an irony that few in the front line appreciated, were far too valuable to be risked in battle, but always had to be held in reserve, a threat that was never used.

A solitary high-flying aircraft appeared from the east. Scarcely a head turned to watch its passage. Enemy aircraft were no more of a threat to them than their tanks were to the enemy. They might be used on reconnaissance, but they wouldn't be risked in bombing or strafing runs on the trenches, where it was far too easy to knock them down with a cheap, shoulder-launched missile.

The most important components of the war machine on this front were the people, hastily trained (scarcely qualifying for the military description "infantry"), cheaper even than a shoulder-launched rocket, and disposable, but burning with a fanatical conviction that this was a holy war, a jihad. The forces of Islam had just achieved another great victory—over the equally fanatical forces of a slightly different religious grouping that also professed to follow Islamic ways and the word of the Prophet.

In Moscow, the three uniformed, red-shoulder-tabbed men sat on the opposite side of the long table from the two civilians. The arrangement of the room could have left no doubt in anyone's mind who was in charge here—the military men sat with their backs to the door, while the duo opposite them were in front of the two large windows, between which a huge portrait of Lenin, flanked by two red flags, dominated the room. Even the position of the water carafe and the spotless blotting pad on the table signaled that the civilians belonged here, but the soldiery were merely visitors. So much would have been apparent to even a casual observer. And yet, as such an observer would soon have realized, the tone of the debate suggested that the balance of power lay the other way. It was the military pressing home an advantage, here; and it was the civilians that were conceding ground, grudgingly, in the face of over-whelming evidence.

"Comrades." The generals were all old men, used to the old ways. The younger of the two civilians frowned, slightly, at the form of address, but could hardly object to it.

"Comrades, there cannot be any doubt about this. When the American forces withdrew, *that* was the time to move. But the Central Committee chose to follow the peace plan. I am not saying that the Central Committee was wrong—"

By which, the younger civilian thought, he means, I *am* saying that the Central Committee was wrong.

"—but the situation has already changed, and it is not changing in our favor. The Europeans have not responded to our approaches, and now they are building up their own forces. There are German generals in command of European armies less than a thousand kilometers from our borders."

That, of course, was the clincher. The younger man knew that the argument was lost. For half a century, Soviet foreign policy had had the primary aim of preventing German armies from marching eastward again. The Americans had always been too stupid to realize this. Nobody in the Soviet Union feared the Americans would invade their territory, but, of course, when the Americans developed nuclear weapons the Soviet Union had to follow suit, in self-defense. Now the Americans had left Europe. Good. Perhaps peace would be possible. But the Europeans were putting Germans in command of their armies—at least, some of their armies.

He had been too young to remember the Great Patriotic War, but the images from his childhood were still vivid. The lessons and pictures, visits of heroes to the school to tell of their experiences. The message had been repeatedly hammered home. We must never forget what the Germans have done to us; we must never trust them, and we must keep a buffer between our homeland and them.

Well, he was more sophisticated now. He could understand that there were good Germans and bad Germans. He could not believe that the Europeans were really contemplating hostile actions. And yet, he dare not take that chance. He sighed, inwardly, without letting his feelings show. It would do no harm to be polite to the old man, and admit defeat graciously. The general was too old to be seeking power for himself, and had an impeccable record; he was surely sincere in carrying out his patriotic duty.

"Comrade General, the evidence is indeed clear. We cannot ignore the threat from the West, and the European military buildup is dangerously tilting the balance. If we are all agreed"—he glanced perfunctorily at his companion, knowing that it was impossible that there would be any disagreement—"then the plan you have presented will be approved by the Central Committee, and you will get your modernization program."

It was only after the generals had taken their leave, and the two civilians were alone, that the older man voiced his doubts, as delicately as he could.

"And the industrial plan, Comrade President?" Only the formal address betrayed the older man's anger.

"Ah yes, Sergei, the industrial plan. Well, the people will have to wait a little bit longer for their color TV and their Western jeans. They are used to waiting, after all; and it is better to have security and no color TV than to be crushed under the heel of the Western imperialists, is it not?"

"And the agricultural modernization plan?"

It was the younger man's turn to show anger, more openly.

"A decision has been made, Sergei. There is no more to be said. The people will just have to make do for a little while."

"Yes, Comrade President."

The incident on the frozen Amur River, just west of Fu-yuan, scarcely rated a mention in the Western media. The Chinese and Russians were always involved in a game of bluff and counter-bluff in this strategically important region, close to the rail line to Vladivostok, where the border had long been in dispute. The river itself formed the de facto border between the two powers, and in winter local patrols from either side would venture out at least as far as the center line of the ice-covered surface, out of bravado, boredom, or under orders to test the speed with which the other side would respond. Sometimes they strayed too far, carelessly or under orders, who could say? And if a group of trigger-happy Chinese opened fire on a group of Soviet soldiers, "lost" in the snow, who had wandered a few meters over the dividing line,

and if the fire was returned, with casualties on
both sides, well, it was all a storm in a teacup.
In the morning both capitals would issue state-
ments regretting the unfortunate incident, the
bodies would be given military burials, and it
would all be forgotten. Until the next time.

Twenty-two

Year Nine

By the time he was eight years old, Adam understood that he was a prisoner, even though the term had never appeared in his carefully censored books or holos. The realization that something was wrong in his world had only slowly dawned on him, as time went by. Infants accept their surroundings as natural—as long as they are fed, played with, and cared for, they will develop happily with no thought of the world beyond their immediate surroundings. But with growing intelligence, curiosity, and the ability to understand language Adam began to appreciate that his immediate environment was only a very small part of the whole world.

He was warm and safe; he had the animals to play with and his own gymnasium to exercise in, and he saw Uncle Dick every day, while Nanny had tended him lovingly over the years. He loved them both. But his world was restricted to four rooms in a single-story building, plus the occasional walk in the gardens outside—walks that were becoming ever more occasional, in a garden surrounded by high fences, with Uncle Dick always close at hand.

What went on in the other buildings he could see nearby? Where did Uncle Dick go to, when he closed the big green door at the end of the corridor and vanished from Adam's world? Where did Nanny come from, and go to? Even rooms, he now realized, might be more interesting than the ones he was familiar with. The birds still held their fascination for him, but so did many other things, besides.

The books and holos brought in to amuse him (and, though he didn't know it, to test his intelligence) showed that there must be many more people than he had ever met, and he guessed that most of them had more freedom than he. Although many of the holos were cartoons and Disney-type features, so that people were rare in Adam's world of entertainment, it was clear they weren't as rare as in his daily world. The sports holos, especially, often showed crowds of people watching and applauding the gymnasts he still strove, with Uncle Dick's proud approval, to emulate. There must be *hundreds* of people, somewhere in the world, he was sure. And although he was neither unhappy nor ill-treated in his prison, he became increasingly determined to escape, out of that combination of typical human characteristics—bloody-mindedness and curiosity.

Of course, he would have to bide his time, wait for a break in routine and seize the opportunity when it arose. But Adam was used to biding his time—he'd done little else for the past eight years.

Part Two
REVELATIONS

Twenty-three

Louise Henderson was at loose ends. As European correspondent of *Research*, the weekly newsmagazine of science and technology, this was a fairly normal state of affairs. The loose ends were generally of her own devising, breaks to recharge the batteries and relax a while before plunging back into the hectic round. She didn't try to cover the routine stories, of course. All that could be handled just as well from Washington as from any European capital, with fax, viewphones, and computer links. What she specialized in, and thereby made herself valuable to *Research*, was the story behind the story—the in-depth interviews, the reasons why people got into certain lines of scientific study, the impact on ordinary people, and, where appropriate, the infighting.

It was the infighting that had got her into this

line of business in the first place. Twelve years ago, a naive but bright, slightly idealistic, young graduate she had started out in research, intending to work for a PhD. The close-up view of the jungle warfare that seemed to be involved in a career as a research scientist had soon helped her to grow up, but had left a sour taste. If Darwin had been around to see a modern university department in action, he'd have needed no further evidence for the struggle for survival and survival of the fittest.

The professors who openly built their careers by publishing under their own name the work of research students, who had themselves to bide their time in order to get the PhD meal ticket that would enable them to feed off the next generation of students; the eagerness with which any new ideas were put down as heresy; and the old, old story of the male lecturers who always made it clear, without being so crass as to put it in words, that good grades could be assured for sexual favors.

She'd never needed to take up those opportunities, but she'd known girls who had, in her undergraduate days. She didn't much care that some of them, with less ability than she, thereby got grades to match the ones she had earned honestly. But it infuriated her that any man—any person—should assume that because she was good-looking she must also be stupid, and in need of such "help." The assumption seemed to go hand in hand with a way of life that regarded all of these bizarre activities as normal. Even the graduate students who saw their work published under the professor's name, with their own contribution acknowledged in a throwaway sentence, simply had not, as far as she could tell, thought themselves hard done by. That was simply the way the game was played— and, one day, if you got to be a professor yourself, why, you could play it, too.

Louise saw things differently. Anything *she* wrote was going to appear in print with her name on it, and that was that. There was no point in trying to buck the system, but when she saw the ad, for a vacancy in the Washington office of the British science journal *Nature* she jumped at the opportunity. She even got a good reference from the professor, glad to see her out of his hair, and stayed for nearly three years, mostly tedious, routine work, but learning the skills of her new trade. And now, after a succession of staff jobs, for the past two years she had been *Research*'s woman in Europe. And everything she wrote carried her byline.

The main attraction of the job was the freedom it gave her to do her own thing—within the limits set by the interfering European bureaucracy, of course. She got a retainer from *Research*, plus expenses, and she was expected to drop everything to do their bidding if a suitable story broke—if some guy in Sussex got a Nobel prize, or a French nuclear reactor sprung a leak, or when the European Space Agency launched another deep-space probe. But she also had the freedom to nose around for the kind of stories she liked best, about the way science really worked, and to feed them back to her boss, Ed Kendrew, in Washington. And *then*, almost too good to be true, she got paid lineage when the words appeared in the magazine. Ultimately, she hoped, her stint in London was going to produce a fat, juicy book, covering the same stories as her articles in the magazine, but in more depth. But not yet—she was having too much fun with her regular work to get down to writing anything else.

Fun, that is, when she could find a subject to tackle. Things had been quiet for a couple of weeks. She'd caught up with a couple of holos she'd missed, been to the theater twice, filed a 1,500-word story from Paris on the interim report of the sea-level study, and now she was bored and restless. She needed a big story to get her teeth into, something that would make a good, solid feature for the magazine, and then form the basis of a chapter in her long-planned book. Good science, interesting people, and, if possible, an American connection. The audience back home, Ed kept reminding her, didn't want straightforward European news, they wanted to know how things over there affected the folks back home. She could do with the extra money a big feature would bring in, too. Somehow, no matter how good her income looked on paper, she could always do with the extra.

For once, the sun was shining brightly outside, and she could see people in the park sitting in deckchairs, feeding the ducks, or asleep on the grass. But she felt no urge to join them. Turning away from the window, she picked up a half-full mug of coffee, tasted it, and quickly walked through the living room into the kitchen of the flat, where she dumped the cold dregs down the sink. A pinboard on the wall held a clutter of mementos—pictures of her parents and brother, one of Tom, a rather faded and battered cover of *Research*, the first time she'd had a cover story, a shopping list, and half a dozen scraps of paper with names and phone numbers.

She prowled round the kitchen, opening the fridge and inspecting its contents, but shutting the door without touching anything inside, taking a biscuit from a packet on the shelf and munching it, turning the radio on, then off again, and returning to the living room, where she sat with her feet up on the long settee.

She needed something topical, but there was nothing good coming up that she knew of. Nobody seemed to have come up with an astonishing new scientific development lately. Six months before the Nobel awards were announced, and even then the prize would probably go to some obscure chemist in Australia. Even if someone on her doorstep got it, everyone in the world would have the story at the same time. She needed to identify next year's prizewinners in advance, then she could really cash in. Like that wonderful book about Barbara McClintock, which was published six months before she got her prize. What timing!

But then, it must have been clear McClintock deserved the Nobel, and would have to get it if she lived long enough. Everyone except the Nobel committee seemed to have known that for years, judging by the other awards she'd received. But that had all been before Louise's time, though she had a well-thumbed copy of the McClintock biography. She really had been some woman—the hassles she must have been through, being a genius and a woman in scientific research in the 1920s and afterward.

Maybe McClintock would be worth a story sometime, if she could find an anniversary to peg it to. It was too early for a centenary piece, and the prize was too long ago for a tenth-anniversary piece, but maybe . . .

Louise swung her feet round onto the floor and leaned forward, gazing vacantly at the wall on the other side of the room. *McClintock*'s prize was more than ten years ago, but who *had* been the recipients then? With all those science prizes—physics, math, chemistry, plus those vague medical and biological things—maybe there *was* one that would be worth following up. How the prize changed their lives; surely some good scope for detail on academic infighting; and she could do the piece nicely to publish to coincide with *this* year's awards. Brilliant!

She stood up and hurried over to her desk. With one hand she hit the On button on the computer; with the other, she was already reaching for the rack of disks above the screen, pulling out the encyclopedia of science and technology. Slipping it into the slot, she punched the code for the directory, setting up a search for information on any Europeans who had been awarded a Nobel in any of the scientific areas exactly ten years previously. Surely *one* of them must have done something interesting in the intervening decade?

Twenty-four

"Hi, Ed, it's me." Kendrew smiled at the recorded image. The redundancy of Louise's usual greeting never failed to amuse him, and roused a warm glow of anticipation. Louise was a first-class reporter and could be relied on to come up with good stories. He settled back to listen to what she had to say, only sorry that the time difference between Washington and England meant that her message had been recorded while he was still at home in bed. It would make a change from stories about the Middle East war and the military buildup in Europe.

"I've got a nice anniversary story for you. Remember Cobb and Lee, those guys who got the Nobel Prize for medicine ten years ago? Well, you can look it up if you don't. Cobb was the genetic engineer, making enzymes to cut genes up and rearrange them. Lee did a lot of the gene mapping, originally because he was interested in human origins. He even used to go out to Africa to get samples from the apes so he could compare their genes with human ones. Kicked up a minor fuss when he claimed our DNA is so similar to chimp DNA that we must have had a common ancestor only three million years back.

"Anyway, nobody seemed to take that too seriously at the time. A couple of journalists wrote a book about it, but it didn't win any prizes. What really made the experts sit up and take notice was when Lee's techniques were used to identify faulty bits of human DNA, and Cobb found how to repair them. They started out with diabetes and cystic fibrosis. Take an egg from the mother, chop out the faulty stretch of DNA and replace it, fertilize the egg, implant it back in the donor, and, bingo, nine months later you've got a healthy baby.

"There was a big hassle back then. Political and religious arguments about the sanctity of human life, you know the stuff. But there wasn't any doubt about the scientific importance of the work.

"So they got their Nobel, and it changed both their lives. Which is where we come in.

"Ed, you'd never believe just how much these guys were changed by the award. It makes the ten years on story really special. First off, of course, by the time they got the prize the backlash from the European churches had already condemned the technique as immoral and against God's law. The prestige of the award helped to counter the worst of that, and reading between the lines I reckon that's why it was made so quickly. For once, the Nobel committee really got its act together. Instinct for self-preservation, I guess. But even so, all that legislation banning experiments on human embryos went through the Common Market, and the courts had a field day deciding whether an unfertilized egg counted as a human being or not.

"Neither of our heroes seemed to have much stomach for the fight. Cobb lit out for the States, wrote a textbook, and ended up as Director of the Cold Spring Harbor labs; you can get Dave to do an interview with him, he seems quite approachable. But Lee went the other way, right into his shell. Moved up into East Anglia, near Norwich, and lives off his income from the Cobb and Lee patents. He hasn't published anything in six years, and nobody I know has seen him at a scientific meeting in five. So—guess who is going to go up there and kick his door down for an anniversary interview? I'm going to call him 'the Howard Hughes of science,' but I won't tell him that till *after* I've got the story!

"Norwich is outside my usual beat, and you know what these guys in London are like processing applications. By the time they give me permission to travel, I'll be too old to care. So I'll go to Cambridge first, on my regular pass, and dig out some background. With any luck, the local cops will give me an extension to go on to Norwich without any hassles. I'll file something in a couple of days, to swop with Dave, then we can both do follow-ups using each other's info.

"Don't work too hard."

The editor of *Research* grunted at her parting shot. All she had to do was run around half of

Europe digging up science features. He had to coordinate the material from a team of such itinerants, and suffer the hassle of producing an international magazine in a format which suited both the electronic publication service and the old-fashioned paper edition that almost half of the subscribers still insisted on buying.

But he remembered the Cobb and Lee story. It had made good copy at the time, with the Nobel Committee honoring the inventors of a technique that was at the time the center of a furious legal and religious controversy in Europe, and was completely banned in many Catholic countries outside Europe. Even many of the subscribers to *Research* (both kinds!) probably weren't aware of how widespread derivations of that technique now were. If Louise could get Lee to talk—and if anyone could get Lee to talk it would be Louise—they'd be a jump or two ahead of their competitors.

Kendrew leaned forward and prodded a button on the console in front of him.

"Tell Dave I'd like a word, would you?"

Twenty-five

It was wet on the road to Cambridge, and a combination of road work on the old motorway and heavy traffic as far as the Stansted Airport turnoff caused delays and left Louise, who had skipped breakfast in her eagerness to be off, hungry and irritable. There was a backup of traffic almost a mile down the motorway from Stansted; when she eventually crawled past on the outside she could see the flashing blue lights of a police roadblock at the top of the turnoff— some kind of checkpoint, they seemed to be checking every vehicle heading for the airport. Probably some new bomb threat from one of the ineffectual, but noisy, terrorist organizations. Or maybe they were on the lookout for someone trying to leave this godforsaken country. She tuned the radio across the bands, hoping to find a local news bulletin that might give

a hint of what was going on, but got nothing
except the usual diet of easy-listening music and
DJ pap.

At least she hadn't set a definite time for seeing the old man. Anytime after eleven, he'd said,
he'd be in his rooms in college. Well, it would
be more like noon, at this rate, and she was
starving. She wondered if she'd be able to get
him out for a meal, or if they'd have to put up
with one of those godawful academic canteens.
But still, at least he'd seemed happy to talk to
her.

Not that she'd actually told him precisely
what story she had in mind; her natural caution
generally led her to be as vague as possible
about the details of her planning. Background
material on the early days of the Institute and
its contribution to molecular genetics, she'd
said, with, of course, some emphasis on the
Cobb and Lee work. And who better to approach, in the first instance, than the newly
retired former Director of the establishment?

Parking anywhere near the college was impossible, of course, and she was soaked by the
time she'd walked from the car through the narrow streets to the ancient archway that led
through into the cloistered interior. In spite of
the muggy warmth, she felt miserable.

The porter was full of sympathy, keeping up
a constant stream of it even while phoning to
announce her arrival.

"Terrible weather, isn't it, miss? The worst
summer we've had since eighty-five . . . Ah yes,
Professor, your visitor has arrived. Shall I send

her up? One moment . . . Have you eaten, miss?"
She shook her head.

"No sir, she hasn't. Yes sir, I'll tell her. Thank
you." He put the old-fashioned handset down.

"If it's all right with you, miss, he suggests
that you meet in the Senior Common Room, and
take an early lunch. Just across the quad, there,
the door on the right."

"Thank you."

Well, so much for eating out. But still, at least
she was going to eat.

A white-haired figure appeared down a stair-
case to the left just as she reached the doorway.

"Miss Henderson?" He extended a hand. "I
hope you don't mind me hurrying you in to
lunch, but something's come up for this afternoon. One of these damned committees. But this
way I can give you a full two hours, and no
doubt you'd like some refreshment after the
drive, hmm?" He smiled.

A professional charmer, she thought. A committee man, all right. I bet he has them eating
out of the palm of his hand. I wonder if this
sudden meeting is genuine, or his way of setting
a time limit on the interview. Oh well.

She smiled back.

"Thank you, Professor. That will suit me
fine."

He took her coat, and handed it to another
porter. No servant problem here, thought Louise. Jeez, it's like something out of the Dark
Ages.

"Sherry?" He had steered her into the Common Room and over to a low table on which
stood a decanter and glasses.

She shook her head. "No, thanks. I'm driving."

"Ah yes. Well. Maybe if I bring mine through, we can find a nice quiet table and get on with our chat while we see what's to eat today, hmm?"

She nodded assent, following him through into the dining hall, where he directed her to a small table, set against the wall.

"Should be nice and quiet here. Very sociable over there, of course"—he waved, vaguely, at the long communal table where a few Fellows were already seated—"but not the place to talk shop, and a bit noisy if you want to make notes. Or are you recording?"

She eased herself into a seat.

"With your permission, of course, I'd like to use this." She pulled the small recorder out of her case and set it beside her on the table.

"Of course. Now, where shall we begin?"

The routine stuff saw them through the main course. How the Institute was set up, the vital contribution (not stated, but implied) of its first, pioneering Director, now retired. Occasionally, Louise made notes on her pocket memo pad, keying the words in one-handed, without looking. They'd help her to organize the sometimes rambling reminiscences on the audio tape later. The professor became more expansive, and more florid, as half a bottle of claret went the way of his pre-lunch sherry. The food, as well as the wine (which she scarcely touched) was definitely a cut above the average academic canteen. She judged the time was ripe to get on to the meat of her story.

"What about the Cobb and Lee work? I see from my background reading that it's just ten years since they got the Nobel Prize. That must have been quite a proud moment for you all at the Institute?"

He paused for a moment, glass partly raised.

"Yes, indeed. Of course, you're American, and if I may say so you were probably too young to take much notice of such things then, but we had some tricky moments with that work. You know the old Chinese curse, 'may you live in interesting times'? Well, those were interesting times all right. Cobb is a brilliant man, of course. Absolutely sound—well, you know he's running things over at Cold Spring Harbor now, really that speaks for itself. But young Richard Lee gave me some heart-stopping moments, I can tell you! Had some bee in his bonnet about human origins, and really got the religious lobby stirred up.

"But there. You don't want to know about that. All water under the bridge, and I don't want to speak ill of the poor man. But I must say, and this is strictly off the record, mind you, that in my opinion he was lucky, damned lucky, to be working with Cobb. Never would have achieved anything on his own. Well, he hasn't, has he?"

"That's very interesting, Professor . . ."

"Call me Peter, please."

"Uh, thank you, Peter. Of course, I'm interested in the work, not the personalities"—like hell you are, she thought—"but after all it is the Cobb and Lee work that most of our readers will immediately identify with the Institute. I suppose it would be nice to tell the readers what has happened to them in the past ten years?"

The waiter appeared, and they both declined the pudding but opted for coffee. He poured for them, then carried the pot off with him. Peter had clearly been thinking carefully during the lull.

"You ought to go over to Bluegene and talk to the people there about Cobb's work. That was what really made all the gene-splicing commercial, and safe. They can tell you how many babies that would otherwise have died are still alive today thanks to the technique, and I suppose they might even be able to find one or two for you to meet. There must be a couple of ten-year-olds around by now, but I doubt if the families would want any publicity."

She shook her head, indicating, if he chose to interpret the gesture that way, that any invasion of privacy was the furthest thing from her mind.

"And I can get one of my colleagues in Washington to visit Professor Cobb. Do you know where I could find Dr. Lee?"

He leaned back in his chair.

"I haven't seen him for ten years. He resigned from the Institute, the same term that they received the Prize. He's got some honorary post in Norwich, but frankly, Miss Henderson . . ."

"Louise." She smiled her most flashing smile, and just half lowered her eyelids.

He smiled back.

"Frankly, Louise, I think they keep him on the complement out of sympathy. Of course, it does them no harm to have a Nobel laureate associated with the place. Not quite so common over there as around here." He chuckled. "But poor old Dick had a bit of a breakdown, and he hasn't done any work that I know of in years."

"A breakdown, Peter? After winning the Prize?" Her right hand was making rapid notes on the memo pad.

"Well, now, actually . . ." He broke off to gesture to the waiter to refill their cups, ignoring the man's presence as he spoke round him.

"Never get a decently hot cup of coffee any more.

"Yes, actually, as I recall the trouble blew up just before the award was announced. Poor chap was actually in hospital at the time. There was a woman involved—well, we don't need to go into that"—Louise's right hand was busy again—"and it was after he came out of hospital that he headed off for Norwich."

Something had clearly suddenly struck Peter as funny—a long-buried memory surfacing again. He chortled.

"Caused a hell of a fuss over at the primate center, so we heard later. Insisted one of their lady chimps belonged to him. Turned out he'd been keeping this damned animal there, for some pet project, strictly against regulations, with the connivance of this woman. Well, she was dead, and he got his way. Took his pet off to Norwich, where they both lived happily ever after."

Suddenly he realized what he was saying.

"Look, this is off the record, right?" He pointed at the recorder. "None of this personal stuff. Just for background. After all, Lee was a good scientist, once. Not in the same league as Cobb, but competent. It's all very sad."

"Of course, Peter." She smiled, winningly, again. She knew, from long experience, that a man like this would regard her only as a pretty face, and an attractive body, and would never imagine for one moment that she could be intelligent enough to pull the wool over his eyes.

"I won't quote you on any of this." But, she thought, I'll use it all as nonattributable background. This story was beginning to look even better than she'd anticipated.

Twenty-six

"Ask Dave to step in, will you?" Ed Kendrew released the toggle switch and leaned back in his chair. Trust Louise to come up with the goods. Start off with a simple anniversary piece, and in no time at all she seemed to have half opened a can of worms. If Dave had the other half of the story, they could be on to a real winner here.

"Yeah, Ed?"

Dave appeared through the doorway—never closed except when the editor was in conference.

"Sit down, Dave. I've got some more stuff from Louise, on the Cobb and Lee story. You know Louise, she likes to keep things close to her chest until she's dotted all the *i*'s and crossed all the *t*'s. But she's condescended to

feed me a few tidbits to see how it checks out
with your end of the story."

"Great. But I hope she's got more of a story
than I have, or it isn't exactly going to be a cover
feature."

"How's that?"

"Well, I've been talking to some people, reading some bits and pieces, making a few phone
calls, you know. Planning on going up to see
Cobb on Tuesday. But he doesn't exactly sound
like your actual scientific genius. He's a great
administrator, no doubt about that. Everyone
says what a good job he's done as Director at
Cold Spring Harbor. And he must be one hell of
a businessman. He made a pile out of the genetic patents, of course, but he's invested
shrewdly, to say the least, and he's worth a bundle and a half, now. He doesn't need to work at
all, but I guess he likes the power and the prestige."

"Strange thing is, though, he doesn't seem to
have done anything significant in terms of scientific work since he came over here. As far as
I know, he hasn't done any real science since
he got the Prize. His textbook, of course—he
made another bundle out of that. Looks like
every science undergraduate in the country has
to buy a copy. And his list of publications looks
impressive on the surface, but it's all light-
weight stuff—review articles, things he gets his
name on as the boss even though other people
do the real work. You know the sort of thing.
About par for a diligent middle-ranking academic. Not quite what you'd expect from a Nobel laureate.

"I guess Lee was the intellectual giant on that team, huh?"

"Interesting." Kendrew pushed his chair away from the desk and leaned back, lacing his fingers across his chest. "Suppose I told you that Lee was a second-rate hack, who rode to glory on Cobb's back and hasn't published anything—and I mean not even a review paper—in half a dozen years?"

"That's crazy. I mean, *one* of them must have had something going for him. They can't both be run-of-the-mill hacks. I mean, some guys can just get lucky and hit on a breakthrough by accident, but that gene-splicing stuff is beautiful. It took care, and planning, and really skillful work, by someone who knew exactly where he was going before he ever got started."

"Yeah, crazy. But that's the story Louise has been getting. Lee was erratic and unreliable, according to her sources. He got lucky by latching on to Cobb, but he wrecked his own career by going out on a limb with his ideas on human evolution. So he's shut himself up in a big house in the English countryside, living off his income from the patent royalties, and never shows his face at scientific meetings.

"And she says there's more." He unlaced his fingers and leaned forward to pick a sheet of printout from the desk. "She says here, 'hints of a disastrous romantic entanglement which may have caused him to flip his lid when the woman died in circumstances nobody I've met will talk about.' She's following it up in the files of the local paper and the coroner's office, of course." Kendrew leaned back again, smiling at

Dave, like a cat with a bowlful of cream all to himself. "Well?"

"Well, great, Ed. I mean, either way we've got a story here. These guys get the Prize and go their separate ways, never working together, maybe never speaking to each other. One is a great administrator and manipulator, but can't do science on his own. He's out front, where we can see him, so we *know* that part of it is true. The other one *must* be the brains of the outfit, but he's cracked up and been forgotten. And a mysterious dead woman—love interest—hell." He stopped short. "You don't think she's making it up, do you? It sounds like something out of Raymond Chandler."

This time, Kendrew laughed out loud.

"Not Louise. She knows more than she's letting on, I'll bet on that, but she won't be leading us up the garden path. We've got to be careful, Dave." His tone was more serious again. "But I want this story, and I want it done right. Go up and see Cobb, and give him enough rope to hang himself. Get everything you can on the old days, and on what a successful career he's built out of the Cobb and Lee work. Find out what he thinks of his old partner. If he really has done it all by ripping off a sick man, who deserves the bulk of the credit, we'll hit him so hard he'll never forget it.

"We can trust Louise to look after the British end. Mysterious women, eccentric recluses. Plenty of color stuff and sympathy for poor old Lee. Might even do him some good, in the long run, if he gets some belated recognition as the senior partner on that work. But the real story's over here—back-stabbing, plagiarism, whatever it is, you get it. And keep it all to yourself until we get a chance to splash the whole story in one go. We'll give these guys an anniversary present to beat all anniversary presents."

Twenty-seven

Louise was tired, and her eyes itched. She paused in her work, sitting up from the keyboard and rubbing at them, futilely, with both fists. It was only mild hay fever, and had never troubled her enough to bother with a course of antiallergic treatment. But they'd been cutting the grass at the back of King's College when she'd walked through from the University Library, and that was enough to set any allergic reaction off, no matter how mild.

She was staying at the Blue Boar Hotel for a few days. As she'd explained to the aliens officer at the local police station, there was no point in trekking all the way back down to London when there was still so much to be filled in here. The *Cambridge Evening News* didn't yet keep all of its back copies on microfiche, let alone computer disk, and she'd had to be on hand to get some of the stories she wanted photocopied. The bored young policeman had been quite happy to rubber-stamp her application to stay for up to three days, noting the particulars from her passport to be filed over the computer wires with London. When that didn't flash any red lights, he gave her a pass authorizing travel within a fifty-kilometer radius, and an official deferment of her weekly check-in with the London Aliens Office for two days.

It was all routine, and dull. Anyone in Europe who didn't hold an EEC passport had to go through the same rigamarole as they traveled about, so that the Aliens Offices in each of the old national capitals knew exactly where they were at all times. Journalists were watched particularly closely—but as a science writer Louise had never been involved in any of the hassles some of her friends at the International Press Center reported. France was the worst, they said. Mustn't blow your nose without checking with the central computer in some districts. But Britain didn't really take all this stuff seriously, just went through the motions to help keep a few hundred civil servants happily employed. She'd certainly never had any application to travel turned down, although the London office was often infuriatingly slow getting around to granting permission. And although it was clearly stated in her terms of residence that if she missed one of her weekly visits to the office, without prior permission in writing, she would be out on her ear, back to the good old US of A on the next plane, she didn't really take the threat seriously.

Anyway, out here in the sticks, you got personal attention, face-to-face. And Louise was used to getting her way when dealing face-to-face with young men.

Her personality worked almost equally well on women. The library had been really good for the scientific stuff, of course, allowing her, with only a little persuasion, to take copies of all the key papers describing Lee's work with Cobb, into the semipermanent memory of her own portable. She'd taken some of Lee's other stuff, as well—the work on human origins that seemed to have upset so many people at the time. But what with the hay fever and peering at the LCD screen on the portable, her eyes had just about had it. It would be nice to be back home in London, with the words shining out bright and clear from the large monitor of her main system. Well, you can't have everything.

Only one thing for it. The itching had spread to the back of her throat, and needed drastic treatment from her own pet remedy. She leaned over and picked up the handset from the table by the bed.

"Room service, please.

"Thank you. This is Room Seven. Could you get me a pot of really hot, black coffee? Just this side of boiling? Yes, thanks. And a large whisky. Okay."

She stood up and stretched, moving over to the bed and picking up a sheaf of photocopies, making a space to sit down. Idly, waiting for the coffee to arrive, she flipped through some of the stories.

No wonder Lee had felt like moving on. This Marjorie Cooper must have been more than just a professional colleague—especially if she was covering up something mildly against regs for him at the primate center. Seeing someone you love beaten to death, scarcely half a mile from your own home, and you helpless to do anything about it. You sure as hell wouldn't want to drive down that stretch of road every day for the rest of your life. And if she'd meant enough to him, maybe the memories of Cambridge itself would be too painful to put up with.

There was a knock at the door.

"It's open. Come in."

She put the papers down and stood to receive the tray, touching the coffee pot lightly with her left hand. It *was* hot. Hooray! She dropped a coin in the young girl's hand.

"Thank you, madam. Good night."

"Good night."

The girl left. Well, first things first. *Hot*, black coffee, to frighten the nerve endings in the throat into submission. Then whisky, to dull the itching in the eyes. It never failed. Indeed, it was almost worth the ailment for the pleasure of the cure—Tom always kidded her that the only reason she didn't take the antiallergic course was so that she'd continue to have an excuse to apply the coffee and whisky remedy.

She smiled at the thought, then frowned. God, suppose something like that had happened to Tom. Would *she* have cracked up? Maybe a bit. But would she lock herself away from the world for ten years?

She drank the first cup of scalding coffee, and carried the whisky glass back to the bed. She had to admit to herself that she didn't think even Tom meant that much to her. She knew her own image was of a tough lady, a career woman first and last. She also knew she had a softer center than anybody, except perhaps Tom, appreciated. She might even give up her career in order to be with him permanently. Well, she *might*. But if he were dead, there'd be all the more reason to live up to her image and throw herself into her work.

Of course, people were different. No telling how this guy she'd never met might react in a situation like that. Lee looked like a nice guy in the pictures, pretty young for a Nobel prize-winner, tall, nice eyes. He didn't *look* like a weak man, easily deterred by adversity. Of course, that meant nothing. But he must have been pretty determined to have got as high up the academic ladder as he had before the fall. And there was that stuff about Africa, too.

She shuffled the papers absently, one-handed, until she found the one she wanted. Field trips to Zaire, of all places, to study chimpanzees in their natural habitat. For Christ's sake, Zaire. She checked the date on the clipping. Even then things were getting pretty hairy in Africa. Made him a bit of a local celebrity for a few days, and even allowing for the newspaper hype it *was* a good story, though probably not quite so much like Harrison Ford's professor in *Raiders of the Lost Ark* as the local press made out. Even so, this guy cared enough about his work to risk his life in Zaire. He'd been, what, forty-odd, never married, dedicated to his work. Okay, he's fond of this Marjorie Cooper. But this isn't Romeo and Juliet—he isn't seventeen, or even in his twenties. Should she believe that because something happens to his lady, he gives it all up and goes into his shell? It didn't fit. There was a piece of the puzzle missing.

She swung her feet up onto the bed and leaned back, sipping the whisky. Something was circling round at the back of her mind. Why *did* Lee go off to Africa? He was a molecular biologist, not an anthropologist. Sure, he said those pygmy chimpanzees were almost human, but he said that on the basis of molecular studies, not field work. He couldn't hope to compete with the anthropologists and zoologists on their own terms. And Marjorie Cooper—*she* knew about primates. If he wanted to study chimps, why didn't he just go over and look at hers?

She sat up, suddenly, and set the whisky down, itching eyes forgotten. Dr. Cooper had been looking after a chimpanzee for Lee— illegally! Where did he get it from? What was an illegal chimpanzee, anyway? Suppose it was there, not for studying but for experimenting on. And with Cooper dead, he'd be likely to be found out—*certain* to be found out, she corrected herself. Hell, maybe he didn't give a damn about this woman at all—he was just *using* her, and he had to cover his tracks quick when something happened to her.

That picture made a *lot* more sense. Wait till Ed gets a load of this, she thought; not that she had any intention of telling Ed about it until she had done some more checking and been to visit Lee himself. Now, what *kind* of experiments would a man like Lee be doing illegally with a female chimpanzee? It had to fit in with his work with Cobb, surely. And that was a gray area of the law, even then. Tinkering with human genes to see how the changes affected the developing embryo. Of course, there wouldn't be much mileage in playing with chimp genes. But there was this evolution business—where was it . . .

She sat in front of the computer again, and searched through the material from the library, eventually locating the paper from *Nature*.

"Genetic distance between *Homo sapiens* and *Pan paniscus*: new evidence for a recent man-ape split."

That was it. Here it was in Lee's own words, stated boldly, matter-of-fact, in the introductory paragraph. "There is now incontrovertible evidence that *Homo sapiens* and *Pan paniscus* share 99 percent of their genome."

The bloody chimps were almost human, he said, and it seemed nobody could argue with that. There was this pious plea at the end of the paper to preserve the habitat of the remaining pygmy chimps, as a tribute to our closest relations. Well, the way things were in Africa today, that wouldn't be any problem. What the anthropologists argued with was the conclusion that the similarity in DNA meant we shared an ancestor with the chimps only three or four million years ago. But leave that out of the story; it wasn't important; concentrate on the incontrovertible facts. If the chimps were almost human, what would happen if you put human genes into a chimp egg and let it develop? You could experiment all you liked on the embryo, and who can say it's against the laws that ban experiments on *human* embryos?

The old hypocrite. "Preserving the habitat of our closest relations," indeed. He'd been out there poaching, pinching a pygmy chimp to stick in a cage at Cooper's place and experiment with!

This *had* to be it. Not a modern Howard Hughes, but a modern Dr. Frankenstein! Oh Ed, she thought, hugging the idea to herself, just wait and see what I've got for you this time!

She sat back in the chair, watching without seeing the words still there on the LCD display. Tomorrow, she thought, I'll be off to Norwich. It's more like a hundred kilometers than fifty, but what the hell. I'll be there and back in a day, and who's to know? Play it straight; get in the house to do the tenth-anniversary interview, then hit him with this stuff, and wait for the reaction.

Twenty-eight

There was no tearing hurry to get over to Norwich, she decided; and certainly no point in coming back to Cambridge afterward. She took a leisurely breakfast, and checked out just after nine-thirty, telling the receptionist that she'd finished her work and was going back to London. No harm in covering her tracks with a little smokescreen, just in case. If she left here at nine-thirty, and was safely tucked up in bed at home by midnight, who could say whether she'd been wandering outside her permitted range from Cambridge in the meantime? Except Lee, and she doubted if he'd be in touch with the Aliens Office.

There were just a couple of references she wanted to track down from Lee's papers before she left. Some work by two guys called Sarich and Wilson, who seemed to have pioneered the molecular-clock technique he'd applied so strikingly to people and chimpanzees; and one by Zihlman on the pygmy chimp itself. So she drove round to the library for a last visit, parking the car at the roadside and walking briskly up the steps, computer swinging lightly from her left hand.

The same assistant from yesterday was on duty at the information terminal—but she seemed surprised and flustered by Louise's presence.

"Uh, Miss Henderson . . ."

"Hi!" she responded brightly, hoping to get in quick before whatever had caused the change of attitude had a chance to sour the working relationship.

"There's a couple of references I'd like to follow up, from the papers I copied yesterday." She sat down, and placed the portable on her lap.

The assistant glanced round, guiltily, as if checking to see they were not being overheard. She leaned forward and spoke, much more quietly than Louise had.

"Miss Henderson, I'm afraid there's a problem about that. I wasn't expecting you back. You see, we've just had a visitor; you only missed him by a few minutes. I thought—well, he *said* he was going over to your hotel."

"A visitor? Asking about me?"

The girl nodded. "From London. Look, I don't know what all this is about. But he had official identification. From Scotland Yard. And he wanted to know about the papers you'd been looking up here yesterday. Uh, he didn't know I'd let you take copies of them. But he seemed very keen to meet you. He knew your name and everything—of course, he would, all the requests from here are on file, and if someone wanted to do a keyword search on who'd been reading papers by certain authors, or with certain titles . . ."

She was rambling, covering her confusion with a stream of words. Louise cut her off.

"And he told you not to let me have any more papers?"

The girl looked around her again. "He told me not to let you have any access to the files at all. He didn't *know* I'd let you take copies. You won't tell anyone, will you?"

She was clearly terrified that what had seemed like a minor breach of regulations was going to blow up in her face into something that could affect her career. Louise shook her head.

"No problem. I'd finished with that stuff, anyway. And I'm on my way back to London, now, so I can get the other material from the British Library—I've got borrower's rights there.

"It's probably some silly problem with my resident's permit. I have to check in once a week with the Alien's Office, you know. Makes me sound like something from Mars, but rules are rules."

The relief on the girl's face was apparent. But Louise's mind was racing, behind what she hoped was a poker face. What the hell was going on here? Obviously her request for the combination of Lee's papers and those he'd written with Cobb had rung some sort of alarm bell, no doubt because she was identified as a foreign journalist. Damn. If only she'd got the girl to request the files as an internal library job, instead of using her own ID. But no, that would have made the girl suspicious, when Louise was trying to appear open and friendly to get favors out of her that the system did not, strictly speaking, allow.

But the stuff was so old. She wondered which of the dozen or so papers could have been the one red-flagged in some central computer. Must be the work on human embryos. Sure, it had been a political hot potato for a time. But ten years ago! The legislation was all in place, now, for good or bad; the gene-splicing techniques were routine medical practice. Nobody made political capital out of that any more, and it certainly wasn't illegal to read about the work. No, let's face it, she told herself. It's the prospect of me *writing* about the work that's got somebody's knickers in a twist. *Why* they're worried doesn't matter, for now, but if they *are* that worried there must be an even better story here than I've sussed so far. I'm sure as hell going to talk to Lee about it before they catch up with me.

She smiled brightly at the girl once again and stood up, extending her right hand and holding the computer in her left.

"No, it's no problem at all. If anyone else comes looking for me, please tell them I'm on my way back to London. And thanks again for all your help."

The girl took the proffered hand, and smiled back, obviously relieved.

"Thank you, Miss Henderson. I'm only sorry we couldn't do more."

Louise turned, and walked briskly to the door. By now, the man from London would have

found she'd checked out. Thank God she'd said
she was going home. In less than two hours she
could be in Norwich and finish her business.
And once she had her story, whatever it was,
they'd never be able to gag her.

She didn't see the library assistant, behind
her, frowning slightly and biting on the little
finger of her right hand, deep in thought. After
a few moments, a decision reached, she picked
up the handset on her desk, punched a number,
and spoke briefly.

Twenty-nine

She'd checked the map before she set out on the
open road. In the direction she was going, the
fifty-kilometer travel allowed by the permit
she still carried, uncanceled, in her case would
take her past Thetford, a modest-sized market
town. So she decided to phone from there, just
in case any bored traffic warden noticed the
London plates on her car and casually asked to
see her papers. It was an obvious place to go
for an outing, stretching her permitted travel
to the limit, and she had no fear that any bored
traffic warden would bother calling in to headquarters to check that the travel pass, issued
only yesterday, was indeed still valid.

It was a good, fast road. She hadn't risked
driving back through Cambridge itself, on the
off chance she was being observed, but headed
out westward, toward Madingley, as if she were

going to join the motorway and travel south to London. Instead, she crossed the route south, and swung right, through the village, picking up the northern bypass which carried through traffic in an arc around the city and on to the east.

The gates of the Institute for Biomolecular Research passed unnoticed as she followed this circuitous route, deep in thought and driving automatically; the trees and half-hidden low buildings of the science park were no more than a blur glimpsed from the corner of her eye. But at the roundabout on the eastern side of town the sign on the turnoff to Stow-cum-Quy and Bottisham registered in her brain, and she slowed a little, looking over to the left at the old road and the cluster of houses, before picking up speed again for the loop around Newmarket. It looked like a nice place, typical English hamlet, nestling in the countryside. Hard to imagine violent murder occurring there—unless you were a devotee of old Agatha Christie novels. But, of course, there hadn't been any mystery about who'd committed the crime in this case, even if they hadn't ever been caught. She shivered, in spite of the warmth of the morning, and turned the radio on, tuning at random until she picked up a music station.

Past Newmarket, she turned left onto the A11 for Thetford and Norwich. In a few kilometers, the road ran through the outskirts of Mildenhall. Now, *that* was a name she knew, from the news broadcasts what, seven, eight years ago? The initial outrage back home when the British unilaterally abrogated the arrangements (they were careful to point out that there had never been a treaty) that had stood since the end of World War Two, and asked their American allies to pack their bags and go home. How dare the Europeans be so ungrateful? And then she'd watched, amused, as the presentation of the story slowly changed, with the returning forces personnel being greeted as heroes back where they belonged, doing the job that mattered, defending the good old US of A. If you asked the average American citizen now she'd probably tell you, assuming she remembered that there ever had been a US presence in Europe, that the President had pulled the troops back because it was a waste of precious resources, that the Atlantic Ocean provided the first line of defense in the east, and that it was no business of the United States to look after the interests of the European Community. As a young journalist, she'd been fascinated by the way opinion had been molded over a span of weeks—an object lesson which counted for much more than any examples she read about in books. And now here she was in the flat country where generations of American Air Force personnel and their hardware had spent their working lives, never once firing a shot in anger. She wondered what the historians of future generations would make of it all.

But already she was coming in to Thetford, with no more time for daydreaming. The station was the obvious place to go. Travelers often needed communications, and she'd be sure to find a booth there—and a car park.

Inside the booth, she set the induction loop of her recorder carefully in place to pick up the secondary wave from the instrument. She'd get

a grainy, but watchable, and, strictly speaking,
illegal recording using this standard trick. It
was so easy, and so routine, that nobody ever
bothered to enforce the regulation against recording conversations made from public
booths, but, of course, the recording could
never be used officially, such as in a court of
law. Not much chance she'd ever want to do
that, anyway.

Louise punched a nine-digit number into the
keyboard, calling up her system back in London. As soon as the screen showed the ready
message, she punched in her personal code, followed by a number she read carefully from the
pocket memo. The call to Norwich would now
originate from her flat in London, and even in
the unlikely event that Lee's phone was being
tapped, that was where the trace would show
her to be calling from. The Thetford link would
only show if her own phone was being tapped
(in which case she was in far deeper trouble
than she had any reason to believe) or if a random check was being made on this particular
public booth, in which case she was just un-
lucky.

The plan was simple. She had to be sure he'd
be in when she called, but, just in case the line
was tapped, she didn't want to tell him she'd be
knocking on his door in person. So she would
request that he clear the decks for an extended,
officially recorded phone interview later that
day, pretending that she would then call him
once again from London to get the story of the
Nobel prize work. When she then turned up on
his doorstep, she'd ask much more awkward

questions, and find out just what had really happened ten years ago, and since.

The screen showed a uniform blue with the one word DIALING in capital letters in the middle of it. She started the tape on the recorder rolling. The legend changed to VOICE CONNECTION SELECTED, but the uniform blue background remained. Damn, she thought. I wanted to see him face-to-face.

"Yeah?"

A man's voice, but no identification. She hoped it was the right number. The list of private addresses of Fellows of the Royal Society was a couple of years out of date, and it hadn't been easy to get hold of it, though it had proved useful on more than one occasion during her time in London.

"Dr. Lee?"

Silence. She plowed on—no choice, really.

"Dr. Lee." Be positive. "This is Louise Henderson, from *Research* magazine. I'm writing a story to mark the tenth anniversary of your Nobel award, and I'd very much like to arrange an interview with you, later today when it's convenient, to discuss your work." She smiled prettily, knowing that he could see her, even if she couldn't see him.

"I realize this is an intrusion on your privacy, but we can do it all over the phone. There's a great deal of interest in your work in the States. One of my colleagues is interviewing Dr. Cobb about his contribution, and we wanted to have your own version of the story as well."

Hah! Got him. She tried to keep the same pleasant smile on her face, not revealing any hint of triumph, as the screen cleared to show the face of Richard Lee. She *thought* the prospect of Cobb getting all the credit would make him bite. But he didn't look as old as she'd expected—no older than the latest holos she'd been able to dig up, and they were all of five years old. Unfortunately, he didn't look all that pleased to see her, either. "Bite" might very well be the operative word.

"So, John Cobb's back in the limelight, is he? Well, good luck to him. I don't know how you got this number, Miss, uh?"

"Henderson, Louise Henderson." Another bright smile, not reciprocated.

"Miss Henderson. It's supposed to be unlisted. And I suppose you thought I'd be eager to put my oar in, get some publicity for myself for a change, hmm?

"Well, you're wrong. John Cobb is welcome to take all the credit and have the publicity, as far as I'm concerned. I had enough of all that ten years ago, and I tell you now, to prevent you wasting your time and mine any further, that I am no friend of the media and I have no intention of making a fool of myself in public again."

Again? There was more here than she had yet found out. Damn. The smile had completely gone from her face now. It wasn't doing its job, so what was the point? She leaned forward.

"But Dr. Lee, I just want to get your own story, in your own words. I promise you—"

"No, thank you, Miss Henderson. You may be an exception, but in my jaundiced view promises from the media are worth less than nothing. Talk to John Cobb all you want, but leave me out of this entirely. I've no wish to talk to you, or to anyone else. And I warn you that if you stir up the religious fanatics with your ludicrous tenth-anniversary story, and especially if you give any hint of my present location, then I'll be suing you, and your publication, for invasion of privacy. I'll hold you responsible for any trouble that results, and I advise you to go out and find some real news to report, instead of raking over old ashes. Good-bye."

His hand reached forward, and the blue washed over the screen once again, this time surrounding the legend DISCONNECTED.

Louise sat back, stunned. He hadn't looked crazy, but he didn't seem to have mellowed over the years. Oh boy. Someone must have *really* upset him, back then. News media gave him a bad time, huh? The threat she dismissed as empty. If he valued his privacy that much, the last thing he was going to do was attract attention to himself by suing her, or anyone else. But what about that vitriol about the religious groups? After all, they'd virtually won that battle, and he'd lost. Surely he didn't think they were going to send thugs into his fortress (if it was a fortress) to finish the job they started by the roadside in Bottisham ten years ago? Maybe he *was* a little crazy. Or maybe he really did have something to hide.

She picked up the recorder, turning it off and folding the induction antenna away, and placed it in her case. With a sigh, she pushed back the chair and stood up. Well, Lee didn't know it, but he'd said exactly the wrong thing. If he thought she was going to sit back and let Dave get all the credit for a story she'd originated, splashing an interview with Cobb when all she had to show for her trouble was a little background color from Cambridge, well, he'd got another think coming. Another hour and she'd be in Norwich. If she had to, she'd break his bloody door down. But first she'd dig up all the dirt she could from the locals.

Thirty

The checkpoint was no more than fifteen miles from Norwich, just on the approach to Attleborough. Oh shit, she thought, as she crested the rise and saw the sign: "Police Checkpoint Ahead: Slow." The flashing blue lights of a patrol car were visible just down the hill on the left, pulled off the road in a lay-by. A uniformed traffic cop, holding a clipboard, was standing by the entrance to the lay-by, watching the approaching traffic, which had dutifully slowed to a crawl, and waving two or three vehicles past while his colleague crouched by the window of a blue Volvo in the lay-by, chatting to the driver. It looked as if it were just a routine, random check; bureaucracy at work, looking out for people with out-of-date documents, or defective vehicles, or, godammit, aliens outside their permitted regions.

She hit the gear lever with her left hand, knocking it into neutral and rolling down the hill at a gentle thirty-five miles an hour. The policeman pointed to a vehicle three in front of her, and indicated that it should pull in to the lay-by. Please, she thought, not me, as she watched the driver obey. But the Volvo was already pulling out of the lay-by to rejoin the traffic, the cop was looking for another victim, and she knew that the London plates would be bound to attract his attention. As he raised the authoritative finger and pointed at her, then in a sweeping gesture to his right into the lay-by, she smiled and nodded, indicating left and engaging third gear. As she slowed and pulled in to the little queue of vehicles she checked the trip meter on the dash. Since she'd selected the speedometer to register miles per hour on the digital display, the trip showed as 46 miles, rather than 72 kilometers. Her ace in the hole—she hoped.

The little line moved forward as the front car was cleared to proceed. Now, the constable was talking to the driver of the vehicle immediately in front of her, and obviously finding something out of order. He had the driver out of his vehicle, standing by the roadside for a dressing-down, while the constable filled out a ticket and handed it over. Maybe that was good news, she thought. If he's got one for his quota, he won't be too worried about me. She busied herself, collecting her papers together—driver's license, insurance, registration document, and the pass permitting her to travel within a fifty-kilometer radius of Cambridge.

The car in front was being waved on, imperiously. The cop looked pretty young—they all did, these days. Must mean she was getting old. She only hoped he didn't think she was past it.

She pulled forward, carefully, stopping alongside him and getting out of the car with the papers already in her hand. That undergraduate psychology course had been worth its weight in gold in her journalistic career. If she was sitting and he was standing, she remembered, it would indicate she saw herself in a dominant position, and that would subconsciously put his back up. But standing, a good head shorter than him, he was the big, hunky male and she was a helpless female. It ought to make him feel protective. Well, that was the theory! How helpless could she appear?

"Good morning, Officer. Any problems?" She stressed the American accent.

He responded to the friendly approach, as she'd hoped he would. Must be bored to tears, stuck out here checking papers all day.

"No, ma'am. Just a routine check." He took the proffered documents. "You're a visitor to our country?"

"Sure am. I've been working in Cambridge, but I got a vacation today, so I thought I'd see some of the countryside before I have to return home."

If he wanted to think that by "home" she meant New York, so be it.

But he wasn't listening. Frowning, he'd picked the travel permit out of the batch of papers.

"You're a bit far off base, ma'am, aren't you?"

"I'm sorry?" A puzzled smile.

"This travel permit. It's for a radius of fifty kilometers around Cambridge." He was pulling

the radio off his belt with his free hand, ready
to call in and check out the credentials of this
"alien" traveling without permission.

"Fifty *kilometers!* That can't be right. May I
see?"

He held the pass out, not releasing it from his
grip. Her hand flew to her mouth, and her eyes
widened.

"Well, I'll be—I'm so sorry, Officer. What a
stupid mistake. The man said fifty, and I just
naturally assumed he meant miles—we don't
use the metric system, back home, and I—oh,
my goodness. Am I in trouble?"

He still held the radio in his hand, but he
hadn't raised it to his mouth. She smiled at him
again, with just a trace of a tremor at the corner of her mouth, wide-eyed and (she hoped he
would think) innocent.

"I ought to check in with headquarters. And
book you."

The smile vanished. "But I was just out for a
run. I thought I'd go to Attleborough for lunch,
it's such a pretty name, then back down the side
roads through those little villages. I was so
careful—I even set the trip meter to see I didn't
go too far."

He lowered his hand, clipping the radio back
on his belt, and stepped forward, bending to
look through the open door of the car at the
instrument display. He pulled his head and
shoulders back out and stood up, turning.

"Ray!" The other traffic cop, who had stopped
diverting cars into the lay-by during the holdup,
came over at a jog. The drivers of two other
cars, halted behind hers, watched with interest
from their open windows.

"Any problems?" He was older, perhaps in his thirties, and looked curiously at Louise, obviously approving of what he saw.

"Lady here says she's made a little mistake." The first cop handed the travel pass to Ray. "All her other papers are in order, but she's outside her zone. She's American, and says she thought she had permission to travel fifty miles, not kilometers. What do you think?"

She smiled just a little, worried smile at Ray, then dropped her eyes, picking at the plain gold necklace, shifting it round her throat. The younger cop was obviously willing to defer to the older man's judgment, so Ray was the one she had to make the impression on.

"Oh hell, Pete, that's simple enough. I still get confused myself. But you know the Aliens Office. They'll have the young lady, and us, filling in papers for hours if we take her in. We're here to find unroadworthy vehicles, not lost American girls—begging your pardon, ma'am."

"Oh, I'm just so sorry. I don't want to cause you officers any trouble."

"Just doing our duty, ma'am."

"Yes, of course."

Pete had made his decision. He handed back the papers.

"I suggest you turn around here, Miss Henderson"—he'd obviously read all the particulars on the license, not just the expiration date—"and head back down to Thetford. Then you can wander off into all the pretty villages you like."

"Oh, thank you." She smiled her brightest smile, wondered briefly whether to kiss them on the cheek, and decided not to push it too far.

Quickly, she was back in the car and driving off, while Ray stepped out into the middle of the road, holding up his arm to stop the traffic so that she could make a U-turn and head back the way she came. She waved cheerfully as she passed, seething inwardly, and headed back over the little hill. As soon as she was over the crest, screened from their view, she pulled in and looked at the map open on the seat beside her.

There it was. A side road, about half a mile ahead on the left, leading down to a lane which seemed to run alongside the railway line, right into Attleborough. She was *not* going to be put off now. She thought quickly. Did she dare stay on the road? If the guy from Scotland Yard checked back to see if she was at home in London, her absence might start to arouse suspicions in the early afternoon. Even if Ray didn't remember the number of her car precisely—and he must have been writing something on that bloody clipboard—Pete was all too familiar with her name, and if they got back to the police station and found an inquiry from London about the movements of an American woman driving a car with London plates in the Cambridge area, they'd be pretty quick to put two and two together.

She wanted to be in Norwich, but not driving a wanted car. And she was beginning to think she wanted to stay overnight, at least, to give her a chance to find out a bit more about Lee's activities before confronting him. Maybe there was a way, semilegitimate. It wouldn't fool anyone who knew what she was after, of course, but it ought to enable her to get out of any criminal charges. She already risked deportation, so what the hell, if they couldn't pin anything worth a prison sentence on her what did another misdemeanor matter?

She pulled the car's handbook out of the glove compartment, and riffled quickly through the pages. Right. A main dealer and repair agency, in Norwich. She checked the map again. Main line railway station, in Attleborough, just up the road. Bound to be taxis in Norwich, and as yet, thank God, you didn't have to show identification papers when hiring a taxi in England. Not even if you were an alien. The way things were going, though, she thought bitterly, it was only a matter of time.

Decision made, she gunned the idling engine, released the clutch, and headed down to the road junction. Turning left, and almost immediately left again, she pulled in by a gate into a field and switched off. Now for the messy bit, she thought. Sorry, car, but it has to be done.

It was a muggy day, and she was sticky and disheveled, having walked the last mile into Attleborough station, carrying her portable in one hand and with a bag slung over the other shoulder. There was no videobooth at the old station, just a voice-only telephone, but that was no hardship. She'd bought the ticket first, and checked the time of the next train, before calling the dealer in Norwich. Terrible noises from the engine, she'd told them, and a red warning light on the dash. Perhaps it was the oil pressure—she wasn't sure. She didn't know much about cars. But there'd been a lot of smoke and banging, so she'd had to leave it by the roadside. She told them where. If they could get a truck out to collect it, she'd get the train in to Norwich. She guessed she'd have to stay the night, anyway. So she'd find a hotel and get some rest, then call on them in the morning to find out what the damage was.

They seemed efficient enough, and as ready as most male mechanics to believe that a woman driver could be dumb enough to drive sufficiently far with the oil warning light on to wreck the bearings of an average engine. Far enough, anyway, she told herself happily, so the crew of the tow truck wouldn't notice the large patch of oil soaking into the earth track by the gate to a certain field—especially since she'd carefully covered the patch with dirt before driving on.

Well, the train was coming. She hefted the portable, and eased the shoulder strap of the bag with her free hand. Dr. Lee, she thought, I sure as hell hope you are worth all the trouble you're putting me to.

Thirty-one

Louise stood in the rain at the side of the quiet English lane, on a damp, narrow strip of grass that separated the road from the high wall that surrounded the grounds of Professor Lee's residence. She had left her bag and the computer at the railway station in Norwich, where she'd changed into jeans and sweatshirt. With rain threatening again, she'd bought a cheap parka in town before taking the taxi ride out to the village, and now she was glad of it. But maybe she'd economized too much—the constant, heavy dripping from the trees was a reminder that the weather had set in for the night, and she wondered just how waterproof the garment was, tugging at a damp sleeve to unstick it from her arm.

She was well aware of the hazards of the situation. But the direct approach seemed to have

failed totally, and even if she went meekly back
to London empty-handed she knew she wouldn't
be allowed to stay in the country. But Britain
was still a reasonably civilized country, even if
their ideas of democracy and freedom of the individual weren't quite what she was used to in
the States. If she was going to be expelled anyway, she'd give it one last crack at getting to
the bottom of the story, even if she had to go in
by the back door. Once she got home, nobody
would care *how* she had gotten the story, and
if it was as big as the attempts to cover it up
seemed to suggest, her name would be made.
Maybe, she told herself, nerving herself up for
the next step, even a Pulitzer.

Dinner at the pub had helped to fill in the evening until night fell. She'd half hoped Lee might
turn up, out for an evening pint, and she could
confront him; but she knew that would be out
of character. A casual remark to the barman
about the big house had elicited only a few
monosyllables in response. She gathered that
the professor didn't bother the villagers, and
the villagers didn't bother him. As long as he
was quiet, and didn't complain to the police
about any after-hours drinking, she inferred, he
could do what he damned well liked. The British, she decided, respected each other's privacy
far too much.

But the pub was now a few hundred meters
away, at the junction with the main road, and
she had no excuse to procrastinate any longer.
Although scarcely out of the suburbs of the
city—she could still see the lights of the new
tower of the climate research center—the house
stood alone, in semi-isolation. She shivered, not

just because of the rain, as she contemplated the task ahead.

Maybe it had been a mistake to phone Lee and try to set up a formal interview. He certainly hadn't been pleased to see her.

She played the recording over as she stood in the rain, watching the flat, two-dimensional image on the pocket recorder until the point where Lee had cut the connection. Then she pressed the "audio record" button, and addressed the machine quietly.

"Well, Ed, as you see, the response wasn't too friendly. So I decided to try the back door, and here I am, soaking wet, about to do my death-defying act and scramble over a five-meter wall, with the aid of a convenient tree. A task made a little easier, you may note with interest, by the fact that the wire on top of the wall slopes inward. You get the picture? It's set up to make it difficult for someone *inside* to get *out*, not really to stop nosy reporters on the outside from getting in. So here I go. I'll leave this thing switched on, so we'll get all the grunts and groans of my athletic endeavors, plus any as it happens actuality of life on the other side. But you'll have to make do without pictures. I need my hands free."

Thirty-two

Adam liked watching the rain through the window. Out there, it was cold and wet. In here it was warm and dry. He felt secure. The fact that the window was not built to open, and that there were bars on it, didn't bother him at all. He'd never seen a window that could be opened, or one that didn't have bars to protect it. Nor had he ever seen the woman running across the wet lawn outside his window, bent double as she hurried into the shelter of the building. This was *very* interesting, and definitely not routine. Perhaps a chance to find out what went on in the world outside—although, to be quite honest, dressed as he was only in shorts and a T-shirt he would rather not set out on his journey of exploration while the rain was quite this heavy.

He was on his own tonight. Nanny was away,

somewhere in the world outside, and Uncle Dick was working in the big house. But he had his holos to watch, and he had the rain to watch, so he hadn't been bored. But he would certainly like to meet this interesting new person who had now disappeared from his line of sight.

Adam jumped down from the window seat and walked into the corridor. Would she come in through the big door? He heard the handle turning, but the door didn't move. Not surprising, really. Only Uncle Dick could make the big door work. The window nearest to the door was in the kitchen. He ran in and jumped lightly up onto the work surface next to the sink, pressing his face up against the glass so that he could see sideways toward the door. There she was. She seemed to be talking, though there was nobody else around for her to talk to. Like the other windows, the one in the kitchen was permanently fixed shut. But there had to be some way to let fresh air in and cooking smells out, and this was provided by a louvered section, at the top of the window, glass slats that could be tilted at forty-five degrees. The slots were too small to allow Adam to get out, even if there hadn't been any bars in the way. But they let in outside sounds, such as birdsong, so they ought to let out any sounds he made. Gently, he pulled the lever to open the slots. The woman looked up, startled, as she heard the movement.

"Hey. Out there. Come talk."

"Who are you? What is this place?"

She took a pace backward, away from the wall, then moved sideways to see him better, glancing back over her shoulder at the big house.

"What's with the bars and the locks? Is Lee keeping you . . . Holy shit!"

Her voice stopped as she moved far enough to see Adam full on. Then she started again, talking much too rapidly for him to catch what she was saying.

"Ed, there's something really weird here. I wish I'd brought the camera after all. There's someone inside this prison block I was telling you about. Or something. I thought at first it was a child, but it's a little man, a kind of hairy midget. He's behind bars, but he wants me to talk to him. I hope this recorder can pick him up okay—I don't want to get too close."

"Hey." She stopped at the sound of his voice. "Too quick. Talk slow, please." He was always having this trouble. Either they talked too fast, or they thought he was stupid, just because he couldn't talk as fast as they, and treated him like a baby. Even Uncle Dick never really appreciated how well Adam could understand things, in spite of his limited vocabulary, if the concepts were expressed clearly and simply.

"Where are you from? Where's Uncle Dick?"

Louise took a pace forward. The friendly tone of the voice was reassuring, and she realized that the figure crouched at the window only looked so frightening because of the dim back lighting, leaking in to the room behind him from the corridor. But who was he? Talk slow, he'd said. And obviously he didn't speak very well himself. The suspicion growing at the back of her mind was too incredible to believe, but whatever the truth there had to be a story in this, something much bigger than the anniversary of Cobb and Lee's prize.

"I'm Louise Henderson," she said carefully. "From London. I've come to see Professor Lee— Uncle Dick." She guessed that the two were one and the same.

"He's in the big house. Working. He can wait. Come and talk. I'm Adam. I live here."

"It's wet out here, Adam. Can you let me in? Then we can talk in the dry."

"No. The door only works for Uncle Dick." The sadness in Adam's voice, and the sudden droop of his shoulders, removed the last vestiges of Louise's apprehension about the prisoner. It was obvious that he wasn't locked up because he was dangerous. *He* probably needed protection from his jailer; Lee was the most dangerous animal around here. Feeling a warm, protective glow she stepped forward right up to the window, and put a hand to the glass. She could see the prisoner more clearly now. He looked almost human, except for the dark hair on the back of his long arms. Intelligent eyes looked back at her, thoughtfully, through the rain-smeared window.

All thought of confronting Lee vanished from her mind. If this was the product of his genetic experiments, she didn't want to be alone with him on a dark night. Christ, maybe he was on the lookout for new breeding stock. But she wanted her story—and she didn't want to leave the little guy—or was it a child?—locked up like this. She'd have to get help. All this *must* be against the law. Whatever trouble she was in with the police, somebody would have to sit up

and take notice when she told them what was
going on. And she could call Ed from the pub
first, to make sure he knew where she was and
got the U.S. Embassy checking into her welfare
immediately.

"You wait here." She cursed herself for saying anything so stupid even as the words left
her lips. Adam certainly wasn't going anywhere, not without help. "I'll go and get some
friends"—if only the local cops will listen, she
thought—"and we'll come back. To let you out."

"And you would, too, I suppose."

The quiet voice from the shadows made her
jump and whirl around, while Adam simply
sighed and settled, cross-legged, on the ledge
behind the window. Lee stepped forward.

"What Adam didn't tell you, since he didn't
know, is that my 'work' mainly consists of
watching him on the closed-circuit TV.

"It is Miss Henderson, isn't it? Your appearance is slightly less dignified than when we
spoke earlier."

"Adam"—he raised his voice slightly—"you'd
better go to bed now. It's late. I'll bring Miss
Henderson in to talk to you tomorrow—if
you're good. Okay?"

Adam got to his feet and nodded.

"Okay. Good night, Uncle Dick. Good night,
Miss Henderson." He hopped down to the floor
and went off to the bathroom to clean his teeth.
He hadn't yet got to see the world outside the
garden walls, but at least someone from out
there had come to see him. The sooner he went
to sleep, the sooner morning would come and

Uncle Dick would bring her in to meet him. Uncle Dick always kept his promises, even though, as Adam had come to appreciate, he only made promises rarely. Perhaps they'd have breakfast together, with Miss Henderson. He hummed happily as he prepared himself for bed.

Thirty-three

Outside, the rain was easing up, settling into a fine drizzle. Louise was debating whether to make a run for it. Lee seemed rational enough, but if he kept a prisoner in a private jail he must have at least some sort of screw loose. If the prisoner was what she guessed he was, the professor must have a whole bolt missing. A minute ago, alone in the dark and the rain, she'd been ready to run like hell, before she got roped in as the Bride of Frankenstein, or something. But here Lee was, at last, alongside her in the flesh. He didn't seem so terrifying as the fears she had been beginning to conjure up out of her own imagination. And she'd come all this way, and blown her London job, just to talk to him in the first place. The more he talked the more story she had, and it was all going down on tape. The prisoner might be locked up, but he didn't

seem too hard done by, and he seemed to regard Lee as a friend. The professor didn't seem
likely to murder her out of hand. She hoped.

"Well, Miss Henderson, you'd better come inside. It seems you've got your interview,
whether I like it or not."

She nodded, and followed him back to the
house.

It was a relief to get in out of the rain. She
hadn't realized how unwaterproof the parka
was until she stood, dripping, in the kitchen
they had entered through the back door of the
house. She tugged, futilely, at the garment and
the sweatshirt beneath it, in an attempt to unstick its clammy embrace from her body. Lee
seemed amused at her bedraggled state.

"You're certainly persistent, Miss Henderson. Reminds me of someone I used to know. If
you'd like to take a shower, I'm sure I can find
something dry for you to wear. And maybe I
could get a fire going—this so-called summer's
been so bloody awful, I've got plenty of logs in."

She looked at him, suspicious, not saying anything. The jeans were sticking to her legs, just
above the knee, where what little rain the parka
had kept out had run off the hem of the garment
and onto her legs. A hot shower was *just* what
she wanted, but the image from Hitchcock's
Psycho intruded into her thoughts.

Lee smiled. "I'm unarmed." He held his hands
above his head, turning to brace himself against
the wall in the approved position. He turned his
head to look back at her over his left shoulder.
"You can search me, if you like."

The image was ridiculous. Hell, if he wanted

to hit her over the head and rape her, or worse, it wasn't going to make any difference whether or not she was in the shower at the time. She smiled back.

"I'll take a chance. You don't look *that* much like Tony Perkins!"

A warm, dry toweling bathrobe, blazing log fire, and a mug of coffee, well laced with brandy, were rapidly removing any lingering doubts she had about Lee's particular form of insanity. Whatever it was that made him crazy certainly didn't make him a mad axe murderer, and his smile was friendly enough. He also looked a lot less careworn than he had on the phone. Maybe it was actually a relief to unburden himself after all these years.

"Well, Miss Henderson, where shall we begin? Do you really want to talk about my Nobel prize?"

She checked that the recorder, transferred to the pocket of the robe, was running.

"Not really, Professor Lee." She smiled back at him. "All this is something of a shock. I've got some crazy ideas, but they sound like something out of a science fiction holo—a wild man, captured in the African jungle, some kind of crazy breeding experiment—I can see why you've kept out of the public eye for so long, but I can't for the life of me work out who Adam is, or where he comes from. I assume he's not a visitor from another planet?"

"No. You were nearer the mark with your other guesses. And it's for his sake that I want this kept quiet. There's no way of telling what would happen to him in the world outside, especially if the fundamentalists got to hear about him.

"I guess you researched me pretty thoroughly before coming up here—not just my work with Cobb?"

She nodded. If he was willing to talk, why distract him with any details of the problems she'd encountered?

"So you know I started out in molecular anthropology, comparing human DNA with genes from gorillas and chimpanzees to work out our family tree in detail. That was the work which led to the detailed human gene maps, and gave Cobb the basis for identifying and correcting mistakes—you know all about that.

"The thing about the DNA studies from the evolutionary viewpoint is that changes, mutations, build up at a more or less steady rate. Not *exactly* steady, like the ticking of a clock, but averaging out to a steady rate, statistically, rather like the way radioactive decay averages out to give a reliable half-life. You can literally count the differences between the genes of two closely related species, and calculate how much time has gone by since they shared a common ancestor. In the case of ourselves and the African apes, the answer is about three million years." He paused, sipping at his own glass and staring into the flames for a moment.

"When we first came up with the figure, the fossil hunters laughed us out of court. They said the fossils proved that mankind had followed a separate evolutionary path for fifteen million years, at least. All that's changed now, of course, since the recent discoveries in Egypt. You won't find anybody suggesting a date older

than six million, and even some of the most
bone-headed paleontologists accept the possibility that the DNA evidence is right after all.
And whether or not you accept the date, there's
no doubting the closeness of the relationship.
Man and chimp are more closely related than a
donkey is to a horse—we're what's known as
sibling species. Almost sufficiently alike to
breed together.

"I didn't find Adam in Africa, Miss Henderson. I found his mother there. She was a pygmy
chimpanzee, a member of the species *Pan paniscus*."

He paused again, and stood up, back to the
firelight, clearly awaiting a reaction. He'd
waited years to tell this story, and it was obvious that he intended to make a big production
out of it.

"But, professor, you can't teach a chimpanzee
to talk. They tried all that in the 1970s. Even if
you bring one up in a human household, it
doesn't have the ability. It hasn't evolved as far
as us."

"Hasn't it?" She'd clearly said the right thing.

"Adam's mother was a normal pygmy chimp.
But his genes are a little different from hers. I
used Cobb's technique to make a few small
amendments to them."

"What about his father?" A dawning suspicion woke in her mind. You could breed donkey
and horse together. If man and chimp were sim-
ilarly closely related—my God, that *would* set
the fundamentalists on his trail, and the established Church as well!

Her face must have given her thoughts away.
Lee laughed.

"No, no, Miss Henderson. There's no human contribution to his genotype either, though it would have been easy enough to arrange. I got the Y chromosome from another chimpanzee. Whim, if you like, but I wanted a male to bring up. But I needed a female to provide the egg to work with. Apart from the modifications I mentioned, Adam is, in a sense, a clone of his mother."

"Then why are you keeping it quiet? If you've found a way to give chimps more intelligence, I'd have thought you'd want the world to know. It's a great achievement."

"But you haven't asked how I knew what changes to make to the chimp genes, Miss Henderson. Shall I tell you?"

She nodded, once again, and he settled back in his chair.

"I don't know how much you know about genetic mutations, but at the level of species as closely related as we are to the chimpanzee there are two important kinds. Sometimes chunks of chromosome get scrambled up in the copying process when sex cells are made. You may get inversions, when a piece of genetic material is literally put into a chromosome the wrong way round, and you may get a clean cut, which splits one chromosome into two, or a fusion which joins two chromosomes together to make one. Either way, the mutation is then handed down through succeeding generations. We can identify the differences between human and chimp DNA at this level—they could do that in the seventies, too. And there are just six important differences, six inversions, that distinguish our genes from those of a chimpanzee.

Six mutations, you might say, that maketh man.

"Of course, there are a few other odd bits and pieces, too. Point mutations, where a single letter of the genetic code has been changed. Things like that. I mapped the whole lot, human genes and those from the pygmy chimp, and I pinpointed every difference. Nobody else has ever done that. And when you look at this level, right down to single letters in the DNA code, you can see which mutations have occurred more recently than others. You can tell the originals from the inversions, because odd bits of code get scrambled up at each end when a chunk of chromosome is turned over."

Lee suddenly looked away from the fire, straight at her.

"You're not making any notes, Miss Henderson. I hope you're getting all this down?"

She felt her face color. It must be the brandy in the coffee, she told herself firmly.

"Uh, yes, professor. I've got a recorder with a four-hour tape." She patted the pocket of her robe.

"Good. I'd hate you to miss this bit.

"The new technique told me a lot more about *how* the changes between man and chimp had arisen. Two of the inversions occurred in the human line, after the man-ape split. But four of them occurred in the chimp line. I wanted to reconstruct the genotype of our ancestors, but I knew better than to try monkeying around with human egg cells, after the new laws came in. So I volunteered Adam's mother for the job. If I could reconstruct a convincing ape-man from her genes, it would confirm the three-million-year date, and a whole lot more besides.

"With Cobb's technique, it was fairly straightforward in principle to reinvert those four stretches of DNA and get a fertilized egg to begin to develop. All I needed was a lab facility of my own, where I could work in peace. The money from the prize saw to that, together with the income Cobb got for us from the patents. He always was a clever ... businessman." The careful pause suggested that several other descriptive nouns had been in Lee's mind, but that he'd settled for something innocuous.

"What I've done, Miss Henderson, is to reconstruct the genotype of the ancestor we share with the chimps. I turned pygmy chimp DNA back into ape-man DNA, and tricked a fertilized chimp egg into accepting it as the blueprint for its own development.

"Unfortunately, I succeeded too well. The birth killed Adam's poor old mother. His head was much bigger than I'd anticipated. And, as you see, he's pretty intelligent. Much more of a man-ape than an ape-man."

It was too much for Louise. It had been a long hard day—the police, trekking out here in the wet, all the rest of it. Her body was ready to relax, though her brain wanted to push on. Maybe that brandy had been a mistake, after all. She shook her head, puzzled.

"But you said you were trying to reconstruct our *ancestors.* I don't understand. How can a chimp's ancestor be more intelligent—more human—than the chimps are?"

"Exactly, Miss Henderson. On this evidence, the ancestral form was much more like us than like the modern apes. It isn't that we've made a great advance, improving on the ape lifestyle and inventing intelligence. Instead, nature seems to have tried desperately to abandon the human lifestyle, as long as three million years ago, starting up at least two lines, leading to the chimps and gorillas, that have lost some characteristic human features, like our kind of intelligence, and speech, and gone back to the forests.

"Darwin got into trouble for suggesting that we were descended from the apes; what I'm suggesting is that the apes are descended from us, and I don't want the news to get out while either Adam or I are still alive. Chimps and gorillas represent a *later* stage in evolution than man, but we've been busily wiping them off the face of the earth for decades."

Was he crazy? How could chimps be more evolved than people? And how *could* he keep all this secret—if it *was* secret.

"Who knows about this, professor?"

"Ah, at last I see the penny begins to drop. You're quite right. I couldn't keep all this to myself—especially since I have to bring someone in from the outside to help look after Adam. Mind you, you'd be surprised. Rumors get around in the village, but it's a close community. I keep to myself, and they don't bother me. A few half-hints about throwbacks and retarded development, and the tragic death of his mother, that I don't want to talk about. Fertile imagination fills in the rest.

"But I'm not going to be around forever. By the time Adam was four, I knew I had a long-term problem on my hands. Maybe he won't live long. Who can say what his normal life expectancy ought to be? But I couldn't take any chances. So, when the government snoopers came sniffing around, following up some rumors, I came clean."

"I don't understand." It was half-true. At least she now understood why her search of the university library files in Cambridge had brought Scotland Yard down on her heels. But why was it secret at all? "I mean, I don't understand why you're in hiding."

"Don't you? I thought you'd researched my background. I had some trouble with certain religious groups, ten years ago. The Church is very powerful in Europe, these days—and I think you've seen something similar in the States. What do you think we should do with Adam and the work that produced him? Shout it from the rooftops that man is actually a mistake, and that the creature that's been made in God's image, assuming there's any truth in that tale at all, is actually the pygmy chimpanzee? I know from experience just what kind of calm and reasonable response that would bring down on my neck, and his.

"Oh no, Miss Henderson. I've got a cozy little arrangement with the authorities. They are supposed to stop anyone like you from finding out what's going on, and I'm supposed to keep to myself. They don't want riots on their hands, they've enough trouble to worry about already. In return, they think they're going to have Adam to study when I'm gone. But I've changed my mind. When I go, he goes—and I'm not sure that I want to wait very much longer—certainly not if this story gets into the public domain."

He stood and picked a log out of the basket to throw on the fire, then crossed to the table to refill his glass. He held the bottle toward her in an inquiring gesture, but she shook her head. The story was dynamite. But how could she use it without getting the mob on Lee's back?

"Actually, I've been a naughty boy." He was standing by the fire again, swilling the brandy round in the bottom of his glass. "Not for the first time. Part of the deal is I turn in anyone like you who comes here at once, with no explanations. But I'm beginning to think it doesn't matter much. It never did, in the long run. But have you been following how things are going out there?" His gesture took in the whole world. "The long run may have arrived, and hardly anyone's noticed.

"It used to be us wiping out the chimps and other African species. Man, the most dangerous animal on earth. But now the tide has turned. We're too busy wiping each other out to worry about them. Have you kept up with the news from Africa? Uganda, Mozambique, even in Zaire, now. Everywhere south of the Sahara civilization has collapsed. The Cape is uninhabitable since they blew up the uranium mines. And in the middle, the old jungle species are making a comeback.

"We've got our own problems in the north. The bad harvests have hit the Soviets, as well as us. They must be desperate, and desperate people do foolish things. This business in Turkey—well, you know as well as I do. We've made it through half a century in the shadow of nuclear war. But I don't see us getting through another human life span. And that means nuclear winter, without a doubt. All life on earth will suffer, except in two places—the deep ocean and the tropical rain forest.

"You implied earlier that you thought Adam might be my son. In the literal sense, he isn't. But in a very real sense the human race was the father of his ancestors. The chimpanzees are our heirs. Evolution has already passed us by, and if we don't manage to eliminate all of the apes before we blow ourselves to bits, our successors are already there ready to take over when human intelligence fails its final test.

"I don't want to be the one to tell the human race it represents an evolutionary dead end, Miss Henderson. But if you want to—I'm not sure that I care to stop you, any more. I've waited ten years for the cycle to turn, to see a return to the kind of sane—well, half-sane—society where Adam and I can go public without either us or them suffering as a result. But I don't see any signs of it. We're further away from sanity now than we were when I was thrown out of the Institute. Maybe the shock will do some good; it certainly can't make matters any worse."

"Dick!"

The exclamation came from a dark woman, standing in the doorway, carrying an umbrella and shaking her hair loose as she pulled off her hat. Drops of water sprayed from the wet ends of her hair as she did so.

Louise glanced from one to the other. This must be the housekeeper—Adam's Nanny. But obviously more than a hired hand; she had to be in on the story. Which way would she jump?

Lee gave a half-smile, and shrugged.

"Pamela, this is Louise Henderson—the reporter that's been chasing me. As you see, she's persistent. Miss Henderson, this is Pamela Barnett. She works for me." The smile broadened.

"Well, Pam, it looks like your dearest wish is going to come true. Adam's going to learn something about the outside world, and they're going to learn about him. I wonder who's going to come off best . . ."

Epilogue:
GENESIS II

The snow definitely wasn't staying so long each year, and the cold north winds seemed to blow with less strength, and reach less far down to the south. The seasonal migration of the tribe reflected this. They were a small band, pushed away from the easier life among the forests and plains at lower, warmer latitudes by the growing population, and forced to wander on the northern fringes seeking food and shelter. In summer, times were good and they ranged far to the north, feeding well and laying in stores for the cold months, occasionally catching glimpses of the bright reflections of the ice cliffs farther north still. In winter, with the coming of the cold, they pushed as far south as they dared, holing up in caves to eke out a more precarious existence while waiting for spring.

But now, they were ranging farther north

than ever before. Even in winter, they could stay in caves as far north as some of the old ones remembered ever having traveled in summer, until the change. There was more land available, and less pressure from the dense population of the southern tribes. But old habits die hard, and still, each spring when the snow began to melt, the tribe would pack up its few possessions and trek northward, behind the snowline.

It wasn't just habit, though. Curiosity, and a kind of bloody-minded determination to push further than anyone had gone before, helped to provide the impetus. Intelligence, which their ancestors had certainly possessed to a degree, had been honed by the harsh realities of the Ice Age, putting curiosity and a willingness to try new things—new foods, new ways of life—at a premium. The undisputed leader of the tribe had gained his position not by being bigger than the others, or stronger, or more aggressive—although, standing a full one and a half meters high, he was certainly an impressive individual. Rather, he was respected for his wisdom, his success in finding food and winter quarters for his people, and his courage in being first to venture into new territory or try new things. Where he led, they would follow—until his curiosity took him too far and he died from eating the wrong food or investigating caves and cliffs that were simply too dangerous. Then, the lesson learned and that particular danger avoided in future, the tribe would find itself led, automatically, by the next individual bold enough to seek new pastures but wise enough to avoid the known hazards. That was the way it had always been, and that was why they managed to maintain the tribe and even increase in numbers, in spite of the difficult environment they inhabited. Perhaps other tribes did things differently. And perhaps other tribes were not flourishing the way theirs was as the weather changed.

It was curiosity, pure and simple, that took the leader into the valley to investigate the peculiar mounds. The ice had been here, dumping its burden of rock and dirt as moraines, releasing meltwater to carve strange channels through the landscape. But the ice had gone, and this was something different. He couldn't imagine any value in it, but his curiosity had to be satisfied before he could lead the tribe on, northward into the greening countryside.

Slowly, he picked his way across some of the mounds, pausing to dig objects that might be of interest out of the soft covering of soil. But it was a waste of time. There was nothing of interest or value here, just as there had been nothing of value or interest in the curiously similar mounds that he had seen before on the tribe's travels. If anything, thanks to the ice, there was even less left here to puzzle over than there had been farther south. But perhaps the detour hadn't been a complete waste of time. Standing upright, shading his eyes against the late afternoon sun, he gazed along the river, down the valley. Easy traveling, there. Water, good places to camp. They were far enough north, he decided. Along that valley they would make their base for the summer, settle down and enjoy the good life, until the snow came back again.

He signaled to the tribe, watching from a safe

distance away. They began to move, down the slope and to the west, on a course that would converge with his in a little while. Perhaps, one day, they or their children, or their children's children, would come back to pick over the mounds and find the interesting things that they concealed. For now, though, the tribe turned its back on what had been the city of Limoges, and looked for a good place to make camp.

BEN BOVA

☐	53217-1	THE ASTRAL MIRROR	$2.95
☐	53218-X		Canada $3.50
☐	53202-3	BATTLE STATION	$3.50
☐	53203-1		Canada $4.50
☐	53212-0	ESCAPE PLUS	$2.95
☐	53213-9		Canada $3.50
☐	53215-5	ORION	$3.50
☐	53216-3		Canada $3.95
☐	53161-2	VENGEANCE OF ORION	$3.95
☐	53162-0		Canada $4.95
☐	53210-4	OUT OF THE SUN	$2.95
☐	53211-2		Canada $3.50
☐	53205-8	PRIVATEERS	$3.95
☐	53204-X		Canada $4.95
☐	53219-8	PROMETHEANS	$2.95
☐	53220-1		Canada $3.75
☐	53208-2	TEST OF FIRE	$2.95
☐	53209-0		Canada $3.50
☐	53206-6	VOYAGERS II: THE ALIEN WITHIN	$3.50
☐	53207-4		Canada $4.50
☐	53225-2	THE MULTIPLE MAN	$2.95
☐	53226-0		Canada $3.95
☐	53245-7	COLONY	$3.95
☐	53246-5		Canada $4.95
☐	53243-0	THE KINSMAN SAGA	$4.95
☐	53244-9		Canada $5.95
☐	53231-7	THE STARCROSSED	$2.95
☐	53232-5		Canada $3.95
☐	53227-9	WINDS OF ALTAIR	$3.95
☐	53228-7		Canada $4.95

Buy them at your local bookstore or use this handy coupon:
Clip and mail this page with your order.

Publishers Book and Audio Mailing Service
P.O. Box 120159, Staten Island, NY 10312-0004

Please send me the book(s) I have checked above. I am enclosing $_____
(please add $1.25 for the first book, and $.25 for each additional book to
cover postage and handling. Send check or money order only — no CODs.)

Name _____

Address _____

City _____ State/Zip _____

Please allow six weeks for delivery. Prices subject to change without notice.

THE BEST IN SCIENCE FICTION

THE TOR DOUBLES

Two complete short science fiction novels in one volume!

THE BEST IN FANTASY